A Game We Play

A GAME WE PLAY

Simona Vinci

Translated by Minna Proctor

Chatto & Windus
LONDON

Published by Chatto & Windus 1999

2 4 6 8 10 9 7 5 3 1

First published in 1997 as *Dei Bambini Non Si Sa Niente* by Einaudi, Italy

First published in Great Britain in 1999 by
Chatto & Windus
Random House, 20 Vauxhall Bridge Road,
London SW1V 2SA

Random House Australia (Pty) Limited
20 Alfred Street, Milsons Point, Sydney,
New South Wales 2061, Australia

Random House New Zealand Limited
18 Poland Road, Glenfield,
Auckland 10, New Zealand

Random House South Africa (Pty) Limited
Endulini, 5A Jubilee Road, Parktown 2193, South Africa

Random House UK Limited Reg. No. 954009

A CIP catalogue record for this book
is available from the British Library

ISBN 0 7011 6820 X

Typeset in Bembo by SX Composing DTP, Rayleigh, Essex
Printed and bound in Great Britain by Mackays of Chatham PLC

For my mother, who has always been there

'All lives are the same,' said the mother, 'except those of children. Of children's lives, we know nothing.' 'It's true,' said the father. 'We know nothing about children.'

Marguerite Duras, *Summer Rain*

I

It is six o'clock in the afternoon and the light is exactly the light of six o'clock in the afternoon at the end of summer – hot and yellow, a veil of red where the field meets the sky.

There is only one car in the car park in front of the apartment building, a blue Ford covered with dust and dirt. The sun hits the glass of the rear-view mirror and slices back, a blade, on to the blonde bob of the little girl standing in the middle of the courtyard.

She faces the field of tall maize. She wears a short, light-blue dress with a frayed hem and enormous pockets. Her legs are parted slightly, her feet planted firmly in a pair of red combat boots with blue laces. Her hands are in her pockets and she is singing. She sings one of those songs that children sing occasionally. Songs that when you hear them remind you of something – you don't know what exactly – maybe of when you used to sing them yourself.

She sings in tune and her voice is pretty. She sings as if she is singing to someone, with precision and patience, neither speeding up nor slowing down. It's the way children sing when they're sad. They sing carefully, as if it is an assignment, a mantra that if you repeat and repeat and repeat it, perfectly and clearly, all the bad and ugly thoughts will go away.

The building is orange. It's the kind of building found on the edge of every Italian town. It has a big car park and a courtyard in front; the stretch of cement is sectioned off by a green, tubular iron fence with two automatic gates that open to let cars through. The benches are green too; the rubbish bins are yellow and round. Lamp posts are positioned symmetrically around the yard and there is a big one in the centre with three heads. There are control panels to open the gates at each end of the yard by the street and their lights flash red.

It's the kind of apartment block found on the edge of every town, exactly the same, except that, in front of this one, the countryside runs right up to the edge of the building.

It was constructed just outside of town, to face the fields. At night, when the lights are on, it's a strange sight. A throbbing box, alive and full of people, in the darkness of the plain.

The little girl sings and keeps her eyes fixed on the far end of the field, the horizon, her gaze grazing the top of the maize which stands taller than her. Her hands deep in her pockets. Her blonde hair lit by the sun.

No one will come today. No one comes any more.

The other children haven't been to the yard or car park for a week. They rush out the main door and take off in different directions. No one calls to her, no one waves either. They don't even wave to each other. Heads lowered, they go directly over to their bicycles and scooters parked together in or beside the yellow bike rack at the other end of the courtyard. They unlock the padlocks in the silence of the early afternoon, pull the chains from out of the wheels, and climb on to the seats. Their enormous trainers press urgently against the pedals. They leave without saying anything. Only the whirr of bicycle chains or the disappearing rumble of the scooter motors can be heard as they move away – tyres scraping against the asphalt.

The little kids stick around, but they don't come down until later in the afternoon, four o'clock, four thirty. They come with their mothers, grandmothers, or babysitters. They're still young. They play with dolls, toy cars, with buckets and spades, stirring up the grey sand in the pit. They scream and shout.

The older kids hang out at the ice-cream stand around the bend, or else they go to the pool. No one stays here.

It seems as if a lot of time has passed. When she thinks of those days, Martina thinks: When I was little. But it was only two months ago, the beginning of summer. Now it's chilly at night. And no one is in the yard in front of the building. The big kids leave quickly, driving off on their scooters without saying a word. Martina has no idea where they go, but she's sure they don't go to the shed. No one goes there any more. The little ones are in the sand pit or on tricycles, with their mothers, or grandmothers. They keep to the back of the yard, over by the meadow, away from the field and nearer to town.

It's strange to be alone in the courtyard. The benches make long shadows on the cement. The lamps around the yard all turn on at the same time. The light shining in the transparent bulbs is pale and uncertain at first, almost blue, suddenly turning warmer and burning orange.

It will be summer for a little while longer. The fields around the town are still yellow. The town: Granarolo dell'Emilia. Granarolo. A teacher once told her the town was named for its grain, *il grano*. Once there was grain everywhere, even where there are houses now. They had to cut it all down in order to build. It must have been so silent at night back then, more silent than it is now. Only frogs and crickets, cats and fireflies glowing on the ears of corn.

The little girl continues to sing. She stands still in this position: her hands in her pockets, her legs parted, her eyes moving across the stretch of maize in front of her, long after the last note of her song has disappeared deep into the field.

Her mouth is tight. Her right hand, tucked deep in the pocket of her dress, clutches a torn shred of paper wedged into a corner along with the crumbs and pebbles. It might be a shop receipt. Or else a note passed between desks at school.

Whatever memory it is, it will be painful.

She takes her hand out of her pocket, her fingers still clenched, then she releases them, one at a time. The scrap of paper, sticking to her sweaty palm, lingers a minute before falling. When it finally drops, the little girl begins to sing again, not once lowering her gaze. The field lies in front of her and the sun falls over it, drenching it with light, swollen and liquid, like the yolk of a cracked egg.

★

For days, ever since they stopped meeting in the courtyard, Luca spends his afternoons in bed, slipping from one dream to another, from one deep sleep to another. He wakes in the morning along with the herd of buffalo that tears through the house for the first hour of the day. He eats breakfast with his family, pretending to listen to their senseless chatter. After everyone has left, he goes back to bed, telling himself he'll get up soon, just another ten minutes and he'll get up. Another ten minutes pass. What would have happened anyway in those ten shitty minutes? Midday comes and he is hungry, so then he gets up, but goes right back to bed, his head heavy from the food and the heat of the early afternoon. The room is completely dark; the blinds don't let in even the slightest crack of light. Darkness and silence. And sleep. To sink into, to drown in, like a puppy or a newborn baby. Every so often he opens his eyes, shifts them without moving his head. He makes his eyes walk across the empty ceiling, tracking the shadows. Then his breath slows again and he hangs suspended like a dolphin, like a shimmering whale in the cold, dark water of a night-time sea, serene and smooth. His mother is furious when she comes home and sees he's still in bed, that he hasn't done anything all day long.

'Are you sick?'

'No.'

'So, what's the matter with you, may I ask?'

'Nothing. I'm tired.'

He shifts in his bed, turns his back to his mother, his legs twisted in the sheet dampened with sweat, his face buried in the soft pillow, his eyes tightly shut.

'I'm just tired.'

His mother stands in the doorway for a while, watching him, then she leaves the room, slamming the door.

It doesn't make any difference whether she's in the room or not. Luca only needs a few seconds of silence to descend back into the watery depths of sleep. While he sleeps, his still body covers itself with tiny drops of cool sweat, a kind of second skin made of water.

Matteo runs. He runs like he has never run before and his coach watches him, perplexed, from the side of the field. Coach scratches his head. This kid used to be like a dead pine cone, he'd fall from the tree at any shift of the wind. Now, suddenly he's an athlete. For the last three days he's been running as if he were preparing for the New York marathon.

He runs and runs, methodical and steady. The bottoms of his shoes beat rhythmically over the dry earth, traced with wrinkles and minuscule craters. He runs with his eyes wide open, staring directly in front of him. He runs as if there is something at the other end of the field, something he wants to reach at all costs. He runs as if he has no choice.

As he runs, his sharp shoulder blades seem to cut right through the skin on his back. His forearms pump back and forth. The muscles in his legs burn, knotting up like snakes. When they uncoil again he stumbles, but he doesn't give up. He sweats like a pig. His shirt is plastered to his chest and back. Occasionally a fly hits his face in its imperfect flight, but he doesn't notice. Then he goes home. Without stopping by the place.

Straight ahead for five minutes through the fields, then keep going straight on, beside the ditch, through the nettles, the purple and yellow flowers, the insects. Down into the ditch with the frogs. Keep going straight, to the end. The tall maize barely moves in the wind. Another few weeks, maybe only a few days, then they'll cut it all down.

2

They used to all play together. Before. There was always a bunch of people: the children from the apartment building and nearby houses, and some who came on their scooters from the surrounding countryside, from Vigorso or Bagnarola, from neighbouring towns. They were the oldest kids, most about fourteen years old. Martina had just turned ten, and so had Matteo.

It was usually the older ones who chose the games, but then they'd all vote on it by raising their hands. They often split up into groups. The smaller ones would keep to the middle of the yard around the big lamp-post – that was their territory. The older kids stayed more hidden, out of sight. They'd usually hang out near the building, by the bike rack, by the field – away from the road. There were a lot of children making a lot of noise. At regular intervals, people would stick their heads out the windows and complain – the old people, the women, the students, nervous from studying and from the heat. Everyone would quiet down for ten minutes, that was enough, then they started up again.

For a while skating was the thing. Rollerblades.

Everyone but the smallest children had them. Martina didn't have a pair, but sometimes Mirko would lend her his skates, stuffed with cotton to hold her tiny feet in place. The rollerblading phase was the best.

Mirko's eyes were green and he had an odd smile. He was fifteen and not much of a talker either.

Martina liked to watch his deft hands fasten the buckles around her calves, she liked his wrists and the pale blue veins that disappeared up into his shirt sleeves. He would kneel on the ground in front of her and adjust the skates quickly. Sometimes, he would let a finger brush over the blonde hairs on her legs.

You'll have to start waxing soon . . . or shaving.

She'd wriggle free of his grasp and push the wheels forward over the cement, building speed. All around her, the other children shouted and clapped their hands. They ran right through the middle of the rink, the brats.

Nuclear War was another favourite game. They divided into two teams and hid, then chased each other all over the block. The secret bases changed every day and the enemy team would never know where they were. They simulated nuclear blasts with bangers that left a cloud of smoke and made the whole yard stink. The smoke would rise up above the lamp post making the air dense, terrifying. They'd all scream with excitement.

At five o'clock they'd have tea together. Sometimes the little ones would come too. In the winter, they would go to the bakery across the street. They'd have pizza, rolls, or cream cakes. When they didn't have much money they'd have to settle for onion mini-pies, in moist transparent paper wrappers covered with blue and red writing. Onion pies were always a little disappointing – made them feel poor. But they would polish them off, scraping the last crumbs from the wrappers with their teeth, licking the wrappers clean.

In the summer they'd drag themselves all the way over to the ice-cream stand, one street away, where the older kids lounged on the plastic chairs, smoking. Or they'd sit on the strip of grass behind the building. At night, it was nice to sit all together on the grass, feet bare. They'd sit in a circle and talk about movies, intergalactic travel, that last amazing goal that put their favourite football team further up the league. Sometimes, they'd just sit around teasing each other. Laughing together in front of the maize field that seemed to be growing right under their eyes, so tall that it blocked out the horizon. The fields were full of vibrations. The wind whistled right through the middle leaving exotic patterns. The ice-cream stand would blast techno music, or the latest Italian Ragga hit, and they could hear it all the way from there. They would dance or look up at the stars, letting their heads loll heavy on the grass. It was great. Even the kissing game was fun. There was a low, western-style wooden fence across the street, in front of a small field. Garish, fat flowers were planted here and there around the fence – gloomy purple and fuchsia. The fence served no purpose, it was just decorative. The little girls took turns sitting behind the fence and the boys would line up on the other side. One at a time, the boys would have to undergo an examination by the princess of the day. If they passed, they would receive a kiss, sometimes they'd even get a little tongue. A fleeting kiss, a smack. Everyone else laughed.

Mirko would lead the way to the ice-cream stand and they followed happily and timidly like a brood of chicks. They all worried about looking like geeks in front of the older kids.

When Martina saw Paolo for the first time, it was at the ice-cream stand, and she fell a little in love. Paolo was nineteen and a half. He was Mirko's brother and had the same unusual eyes, but Paolo talked a lot. Paolo liked Martina too. He had said to her, 'When your tits grow . . .' After that, Martina would look at herself in the mirror every night before going to bed. But her chest was always flat, calm. Calm like the stretch of fields outside her window, like the grand old houses in the distance.

Martina thinks about how it used to be, before. She thinks about her mother leaning over the balcony to call her in. About all the times she would race down the stairs, not stopping to wait for the lift, so that she could get to the bench on the opposite side of the yard in time, the bench by the lamp post, where the others were waiting for her.

The big kids would drive their scooters in circles through the middle of the yard. They drove slowly, making figure eights around the lamp posts and the telephone booths.

She would go down at nine and come back at ten thirty. Without fail. Nine to ten thirty. There was a lot of time between nine and ten thirty, time to disappear and come back again.

The mothers watched the crowd of children down in the courtyard from the windows. It made them happy to see the children running and shouting, never too far away.

They didn't worry – with all those children, all of them out there together. The mothers trusted a group. They had faith in the other mothers. If one of them got distracted or wasn't looking, there was always someone else there watching out for all the kids.

The little children make a racket. Laughter from the ice-cream stand around the bend floats back to the yard. The old people walk arm in arm and then collapse exhausted on the benches. But her friends aren't here. Not any more.

Surely something will happen now. Someone will start asking questions, try to find something out. Someone has got to come. They have to.

Everyone has left. Even the other kids, the ones who don't know anything. They sense the ugliness in the wind and so they stay away.

Today, Matteo thought about calling Martina. He had just got back from practice, still breathless, his lungs aching from all the running. His mother was in the shower. When he went over to the telephone he remembered he didn't know Martina's telephone number. They had never called each other; there had never been any reason to. But now he wanted to hear her voice. He wanted to hear the phone ring two, or three times in the emptiness, and he wanted to hear that soft steady voice say 'Hello?'

He'd have to look the number up in the phone book. It was probably under her mother's last name, which he didn't know. He could get the phone book from the bottom drawer in the kitchen. Leaf through the thin paper, turning the pages one at a time, run his index finger down that infinite procession of names listed in alphabetical order. A wave of nausea hit him: the smell of ink and paper. And his mother came out of the bathroom. What would he say to Martina anyway? Nothing. Hear her voice. Hang up, his heart pounding in his chest.

What has he just eaten? He doesn't know; doesn't remember.

For the last three or four nights Matteo has eaten whatever his mother puts on his plate without noticing what it is. He digs his fork in and lifts it to his mouth, his head hanging over his plate and his eyes dull.

When his stomach swells and begins to ache, when he feels like he is about to throw up, he starts wondering. He looks at his mother and tries to figure it out from her face. What has she put on his plate? If she'd only give him a signal, a clue – ask if he liked the fish, whether there was enough sauce on the pasta – then he'd calm down. He'd be able to run his tongue around his mouth and capture whatever the taste was, the disappearing taste. He'd be able to say to himself: I ate fish; I ate pasta with meat sauce. Then the world would make sense again. They would all go back to how it was before. But that doesn't happen. She keeps quiet and watches him, her expression sweet and tired. She waits for him to finish so she can clear the table and put the kitchen in order – in silence.

Last night he went to the bathroom, locked the door, stuck his hand in his mouth, tickled his tonsils and made himself vomit. He had to shove his hand all the way to the back of his mouth, scratching his palm with his front teeth, so that he could empty himself out. It was green, spongy vomit. Spinach. Now he could relax. He had eaten spinach. He used to like spinach a lot when he was little.

His mother had told him about Popeye, a cartoon from her own childhood. Popeye, the sailor, covered with tattoos, a pipe in his mouth. All Popeye had to do was squeeze open a can of spinach with his fist and squirt it into his mouth and it made him instantly super strong and then he could destroy the bad guys.

Martina stares at her plate, not raising her eyes once. All three of them are silent. Her mother gets up to change the plates for the second course. She sets the pan down, smoothing out the tablecloth under it with dry, nervous little pats. Her father lifts his fork to his mouth, quickly, rhythmically. The gestures spin before her, make her head ache: hands lift the grated cheese, lift the salt and pepper, lift the water bottle, tear a piece of bread, mix, cut, mix again, move things.

Dinner tonight is fried eggs and mixed salad. They use the black and white flowered tablecloth and the glasses with the tall stems that are too easy to knock over and break. Martina eats without stopping to breathe. Her parents don't say much either. They look tired. To tell the truth, they always look tired, and they never seem to have any time. No one ever has much time, not even the children.

But they did. Martina and her friends. Time is what they did have.

After eating, she goes back to her room, closes the door, and sits at her desk.

It's useless to pretend there's anyone down in the court-yard. She can hear the rumble of the scooters gathered at the ice-cream stand. But it isn't her friends.

Outside, a breeze moves the maize in the field and the shadows lengthen on the strip of land in front of the building. Dense shadows.

Martina leafs through her composition notebook from last year. There are drawings at the end of every essay and a grade marked in the teacher's red pen. Very good. Good Work. Descriptive ability. Pay more attention to punctuation!

There are more drawings between the pages. A dog locked up in a cage, a blue flower in a jar, a heap of rubbish with seagulls flying in circles around it, a red and blue chimney.

Good! You show much imagination – in your artwork, too!

She continues reading, leafing through the pages of the notebook, but can't seem to stay focused. Her eyes keep shifting up and out the window, trying in the darkness to cross the immense field, and reach the end.

Cross the fields, through the dark, eyes peeled so you can make out the paler strips of earth between the crops. The ditches, the irrigation canals. The white canvas covering the delicate plants: huge milk-coloured caterpillars with bloated stomachs.

3

Up until last year, Martina's mother would help her with her bath. She'd fill the tub with hot water, measure the temperature with her hand and push Martina in by her shoulders. She'd soap her all over with a sponge, always the same sponge – the same brand; big, pink, lots of holes, soft – scrubbing hard over the entire surface of her body.

In the meantime, Martina would look out the window. The window in the bathroom was narrow and high; you could only see the sky out of it. She'd fix her eyes on the bare glass, no curtains, while her mother would repeat the same, identical movements, week after week, practical and impersonal. Lather up, scrub, use one hand to rinse off, rinse again, more carefully, getting all of the hidden places, polishing all the corners attentively, knees and elbows, always encrusted with dirt and dust.

She remembers her mother sometimes sang, songs without words, songs that slid from her throat – the sound measured and peaceful, absent-minded. Martina would look out: a cloud, two clouds, three clouds, a bird, two, three, rain, snow, dark, light.

Afterwards, cloaked in a swirl of talcum powder, she'd

sit and wait on the closed toilet seat for her mother to bring her clean clothes, and she'd look in the mirror, cloudy with steam. She never expected anything from her body and she never looked at herself. She'd watch the sky in the mirror and listen to her mother's voice, waiting for the invasion to be over.

It's different now. Martina takes her bath alone, the door closed and locked despite her father yelling and her mother protesting. The water is almost cold, summer and winter – no more clouds of steam, of talcum powder. She explores her skinny body with suspicion in the mirror: transparent skin, bones jutting out, belly ever so slightly rounded, thin legs, the soft triangle of smooth, hairless flesh between her thighs – the triangle slashed down the middle that she has obsessively reproduced, drawn with thick felt markers under the skirts of every one of her dolls, even Malfalda, the hand-me-down doll from her mother's own childhood.

On the bathroom shelf there's a small bottle of diorissimo. Her mother's perfume. It has always been the smell of this bathroom, this window, this open view of the sky. Musk. A simple, white perfume. So good it knocks you out. Always: the smell of her ten years. The smell of the whole story.

Even though there's no school now, Martina wakes up with her parents and has breakfast with them.

Sitting in silence on her chair, the one that faces the window, tucked between the refrigerator and dishwasher, she looks at the boxes lined up on the table: cocoa pops, honey puffs, special k, all bran. Coloured cardboard boxes, decorated: a bear dressed up like a milkman, a lion with a hat, a tough-guy tiger, a woman in a red swimsuit jumping on a beach. Everything's there: the plate with the butter to spread on toast, the milk carton already opened and in its canary-yellow plastic container, the regular sugar and the brown sugar in two white bowls, the sweet'n low, different sized mugs for milk, coffee, ovaltine. Spoons. A jar of orange marmalade, different coloured tea bags in a little bowl. Her mother never forgets anything.

Martina rests her arms on the table, as if to protect her mug. She's not hungry. There's a soft weariness in her eyes, almost gluing them shut. Her head is thick with monstrous dreams: ships in flames stranded on the beach, giant fish with gaping jaws rising from the black water. Too many cartoons, or, maybe, too much darkness – absorbed while looking at the black fields out her window at night before going to sleep. The mournful sound of the combine harvesters that have just started to cut the fields, strip them, runs all night long, or at least until she falls asleep. Afterwards there will be piles of empty dirt. Grey, naked earth; so much space all around.

In the morning, when the maize moves wildly in the wind, a beautiful and frightening sound comes into the room. It's like a voice. Martina wakes and this voice is whispering around her, floating in through the window. It's always been like this, but this year more so. This summer has been different.

It's become difficult to fall asleep. Continuous flashes of light cross her closed eyes, details swell until they explode inside her. Hours and hours, lying still in bed, trying to let everything go, to forget, to neutralise those painful strokes in her eyes. It's so hard. But sleep finally comes. It comes suddenly and her mattress seems to open up, splits in half so that she can fall into a silent place where her body is carried weightless, wrapped in the sheets. The fall is long and she never hits the ground.

But it's better to stay awake – despite everything. The night is full of holes. Sometimes it seems as if roads are opening up beyond the fields, forming unexpected pits you might fall into and never get out of – fall in, just looking at them.

Everything leaps on to her at night, materialising in the dark. Her mother's words, the line over her father's forehead when he's tired, the kind gestures she wanted to make, but didn't. Matteo's eyes: some mornings at school, looking out the window instead of playing outside with his friends. Greta's little arms on the desk. Mirko's eyes shut tight tight, as if he is crying. All of the wickedness of the people around her, of people she loves, descends on to her, passes over her – thousands of feet and hands. A huge, heavy truck, crushing her under its enormous wheels. As if it were her fault. As if she could do anything about it, make it go away, make the wickedness go away, fly away like dust. But she's only ten years old, and at ten you can't do much of anything.

Martina doesn't have a best friend. She never has had. Friends come and go. They last one season, and then get bored. She is never alone with anyone. She prefers to be in a group. You can hide in a group, you can keep quiet and nobody notices. Just laugh at everyone's jokes, follow them when they move, stop when they stop. It's easy. Like being alone in your room.

Martina's room is small. The windows open out on to the fields. Her books are spread over the bed, the older dolls tossed into the corner, little monsters with their hacked-off hair, scribbled over with fluorescent markers. The newer dolls are arranged on the shelf.

She sits on the bed, amid the scattered books, silent, hands crossed behind her head, eyes fixed on the blue line of sky outside. Her parents' voices mingle with the voices on TV – that pathetic talk-show host, the stupid announcers, her father's voice raised and her mother complaining. But she's here, with her scattered books and the music. Alone.

One summer, when Martina was very small, there was Cristina. Cristina had blue, doll's eyes, and was always carrying around a pink satchel with Barbie clothes inside. She'd lay the clothes out on the pavement on a piece of fabric and say, 'Now we'll have a shop.' But then she'd tire of the game immediately and would fold the clothes back up perfectly and pack them away in the satchel.

Cristina knew a lot of stories and would tell them to the smaller kids, who gathered around her and her doll's clothes, sitting on the ground to listen. Cristina left; she said she was going somewhere to live with her mother – Turin, no, to Genoa. There's no beach in Turin.

The little kids grew up and forgot all of Cristina's stories. Now they are the older ones, and they tell the little kids stories from some comic book – a Dylan Dog adventure – or the girls might describe an episode of *First Kiss* or *Baywatch*. But the little kids are too little and they get bored. They want to hear story stories, and the big kids don't know any.

Her mother only calls her once. One call, loud and sharp: Martina! And she has to come right away. At home, the TV is always on. Channel 5 in the evening, over dinner, then the weekly news round-up after that. Martina watches her father laugh at the TV. Nothing makes her laugh. The egotistical, red-faced talk-show host. The music, all trumpets and drums. Vomit. But he keeps laughing.

Two months ago, he told her to stop wearing her combat boots, it had got too hot, they were unhygenic. That's what he said. So Martina wore her leather sandals with the buckles, the kind with a smooth sole that slides over the ground and makes you trip. When she got out on to the landing, she'd take them off and pull her combat boots and sweaty sports socks out of her backpack and put them on instead.

Martina! One call and that's it. But now it's different. Now Martina doesn't always remember to change her shoes on the landing. She stands in front of the door, her backpack on her shoulders, and tries to remember what she's supposed to do. But her thoughts get trapped, and drift away. They go back to the place. Now, sometimes, she'd like to escape into the middle of the fields, go inside, and disappear.

Straight through the fields for five minutes. Keep straight, following the distant outline of the factory to your right. Keep going straight, into the ditch, with the frogs and crickets. In through the middle of the nettles, the yellow and purple flowers. All the way to the end.

4

Mirko arrived one afternoon, about five months ago, in April, with something hidden under his jacket. All the older kids huddled round him: a secret gathering. The little kids were over by the bench, talking about dog food, and didn't even look up. Balancing on one combat boot, like a crane, Martina stood between the two groups. Undecided. Greta came over and shoved her gently but didn't make her fall. She shot Martina her famous Smile, the smile that had charmed the whole apartment building – so much so, that Greta was always the one sent to make apologies and beg forgiveness from the grannies. Martina looked her in the eyes – doll's eyes, too, like Cristina – and smiled back. Last year, during the Christmas break, Greta had invited her over to help make decorations for the main door of the building. Across the big table at Greta's house, over coloured markers, tissue paper, scissors with round points and tubs of glue, Martina's hand brushed Greta's hand: a moment. It was simple, it just happened, for no reason. Greta smiled her Smile. And Martina had thought that, even though Cristina was gone, she still might be able to have a friend, someone to trust again. But

Greta smiled for everyone. The same smile for everyone.

The big kids talked for a few more minutes, then headed over to the corner where the bicycles and scooters were parked and took off, motors roaring, dust flying, shouting out last-minute directions. Martina watched their shadows grow small down the road heading into the country. They were probably going to the secret hide-out, an abandoned shed a few miles away, where the girls and little kids had never been invited.

A mysterious ritual began that afternoon. An appointment. It didn't happen every day; but when Mirko arrived, an odd expression on his face, the others would gather around him for a few minutes, then they would all leave together for the shed. They crowded into a circle, shoulder to shoulder, heads touching, and the words they exchanged got trapped inside. A quick nod from Mirko and they'd all jump on to their scooters. Their faces were almost savage, as if they were conspirators. They'd look over their shoulders nervously, to make sure no one was watching.

These group disappearances kept on for about two months, then something happened. The group split up and most of the boys went back to whatever they were doing before. Still with Mirko – loyal because they had been chosen – were Luca, just fourteen, and Matteo, ten.

Martina never knew what had happened to make a group of three when before there had been so many. No one ever discussed it. Maybe, it was simply because the others weren't interested in what Mirko had in mind, maybe they were bored, or they weren't ready, or right.

★

Matteo was in the fifth year too, but in a different class. His classroom faced Martina and Greta's. The two classes were twins. Having a twin class was the teacher's big idea. She never stopped talking about it; it was her obsession.

Even their town, she would explain, had a twin town in France. It was a charming little town and soon the children from that school would come for a visit.

But no one ever came and none of them could remember the name of the twin town, lost somewhere in the French countryside.

5-E and 5-F really were twins. They took field trips together, went to the theatre, to museums. 5-E, 5-F. They were united by the letters they brought home and by the warnings and complaints about trouble-making: since the first year, the two classes had always been the most unruly in the whole school.

All year long, Matteo stayed in at playtime and stared out the window. He'd look at the playground, the two yellow slides, the colourful roundabout, the green wood jungle-gym with its moulded swings and main pole painted orange. There were big trees all around. The pizzeria across the street had a red and yellow sign. Cars passed by, or stopped at the crossroads. He stared. Sometimes he'd flip through a comic book and eat his packed lunch, or draw in his notebook. The whole year, he never went out to the playground with his classmates. He hadn't always been like that. In the past, he'd be in the gym during the winter, the playground in the summer, playing ball, mucking around with the others. He didn't feel like doing that any more. His words got stuck somewhere, deep inside him. It would have been exhausting to go out with the others, to choose words that would fit into the discussion, to tone his voice to suit those words, keep track of the jokes, to laugh. He didn't want any of it. Instead, he stayed inside, letting his eyes slide effortlessly over the shapes outside the window, watching the flashing indicators of the cars and the heavy branches waving on the other side of the glass.

For a few months, Greta and Martina would come looking for him. Right after the bell rang and the classroom doors opened, they'd come running over to stick their heads through the door of 5-E, calling to him, as they'd always done, every year. He would turn, try to smile, but then he'd go red and they'd flee, embarrassed by his shyness. After a while, they stopped coming. Forgot about him.

Afternoons in the front yard were another thing entirely. Mirko was in charge there. And if Mirko had chosen him, included him without hesitation in the inner circle, there must be a reason. Matteo was the only one of the little kids to have the privilege of riding on the back of Mirko's scooter and being part of the secret games at the shed.

It might have been precisely because he could keep quiet; because words didn't attach themselves to him – they slid off. His silence, like Martina's, was a deep, dark water where lots of things floated. All of them silently.

Mirko didn't talk much either, but his silence was different. He gave curt, precise orders. No explanations. His voice was direct, stern, toneless – metallic, like those automated voices on the telephone. Maybe his voice was changing, and he hadn't yet figured out how to control it.

Luca talked a lot. He told jokes, he made fun of everything. Luca was always on in the background, like a blaring radio. Even at home, just after he was born, his wailing and singing could be heard through the whole neighbourhood.

Luca and Mirko had one fight about Matteo. Luca thought they should keep the little kids out and Matteo was a little kid. He was too young, and everyone knows little kids talk. They always blab everything, they can't keep their mouths shut. It was dangerous. It wasn't the same as with the others. They did stuff together, had fun. So, they'd all gone off for some reason – but it wasn't like anybody was going to talk. As for the girls – well, they needed girls there, of course, it wouldn't be fun for very long without them. Girls might tell, too, that's true. But you could always frighten them, threaten them. Girls are just happy to be getting attention from older boys. But a stupid little boy like Matteo? Why was he there anyway? What were they going to do with him?

The two of them were in the yard, sitting on a bench. The other children were running around, chasing each other and yelling.

Mirko let Luca talk for a good five minutes, listing the possible damage that Matteo's presence might cause. Then he shut him up, abruptly. His expression didn't leave room for challenge. Discussion over. Matteo was in. End of story. Luca was pissed off for two minutes; then he got over it.

Luca had an older sister he liked to spy on. He had been doing it for ever. He couldn't remember a single day, from when he was first old enough to understand about girls,

31

that he wasn't planning ambushes, setting traps, waiting. His sister was six years older. And one summer day, without warning, after Luca had been spying on her for years and years and hadn't noticed anything changing, she got tall and beautiful, with light blonde, curly hair and gigantic tits. From that day, she started to go out with a succession of boys. She'd sit in cars with them in front of the house at night and kiss. Luca would hide at the edge of the window, positioned so he could watch her. He outdid himself once: he hid in the rear of the hatch-back to follow her, secretly, on a date with her boyfriend of the moment. When she tilted back the seat to get more comfortable, she saw him and chased him out of the car into the fields, brandishing a long stick she had every intention of cracking over his arse.

Having an older sister to spy on means you learn a lot. Luca got the whole menstruation deal right away, and got it better than the others. He pilfered tampons from the bin in the bathroom so he could check chromatic and olfactory variations through the cycle. He wanted to make sure it really was blood and, if it wasn't, what it was.

Having an older sister gives you access – days, months, years of access – to her underwear drawer. You know bra and knicker sizes by heart; you have a precise, even empirical notion of what a pussy is like. In every phase: without hair, with some hair, with a real bush, waxed, shaved.

Maybe that's why Luca was never scared.

5

Martina and Greta were invited along one afternoon. Mirko's tone was solemn, formal. He said there were things girls should know about too, and asked if they wanted to go to the shed.

He didn't have to say another word. Without bothering to answer, Martina had already jumped on to the back of his scooter. Her eyes were bright and restless. But Greta whimpered, smirked, asked questions, wanted details. Then, realising she didn't have any choice in the matter – it had already been decided – she climbed on to the back of Luca's scooter and wrapped her arms around his waist. When she swung her leg up, her yellow dress lifted and, for a fraction of a second, you could see her knickers, white with lace trim.

Matteo followed on his bicycle, leaning into the pedals, his calves firm and long, taut with the effort, his sweaty hair clinging to his neck. The red baseball cap he always wore was planted on his head. He lifted his bottom up off the seat in order to push harder.

A lot of different things went through Martina's head during that scooter ride – around the soft bends in the road, the yellow and green fields in her eyes. She remembered a dream she'd had. She and Mirko were running down the hallway at school, it was night, they were being chased by someone, and there was a window high up with a strange light coming through. Mirko grabbed her hips and lifted her to the window. She looked out and the outside was an inside, a room with marble columns and a swimming pool in the middle. The water was deep blue, fake. She thought about Greta, her Smile, her hand soft and warm under her own and the secret little triangle under her yellow skirt. Then a thought flashed into her mind: to be in the middle of the fields at night with Mirko and not be ten years old.

The shed sits in the middle of a clearing in a field of herbs, quite far out from the town, on the way to Vigorso. It's five minutes away by scooter, fifteen or twenty by bicycle. Outside there is a whole slew of different kinds of wheel tracks on the ground; an improvised bonfire made of brushwood and dry branches, surrounded by blackened rocks; broken bottles, rubbish. Inside: pillows, rugs spread over the bare floor, a warped and wobbly table, a ghetto blaster, half-burned candles in a ceramic plate. There's an enormous bed made up of three different-sized mattresses jammed together. Scraps of mismatched sheets and coloured blankets on top. The only window is high up, in the middle of the back wall. It's the window from the dream.

They had brought all this stuff in the beginning, when a lot of them used to come and they had grandiose ideas about how to transform the dump into some kind of Party House. There's a place nearby where people leave old mattresses, chairs, stuff they're throwing away. It's in a lay-by on the road to Vigorso, at the crossroads before the hospital. When you pass it, there's always something there. The next day it's gone and has been replaced by something else. It's a kind of secret resource for people who don't have much money. They had got everything from there. Paolo, Mirko's brother, had brought the mattresses in his car. In exchange for the favour, he sometimes comes to have sex with his girlfriend and he makes everyone clear out for a few hours. And, yes, they clear out – go behind the shed, eavesdropping and, if they can work it, spying through a crack in the wall.

Paolo's girlfriend never takes off all her clothes. Once they watched her sitting on the table, spreading her legs, hitching up her skirt and squeezing Paolo's hips with her thighs while he moved against her. They always kiss a lot and laugh. They seem to have fun, as if, as long as they're together, they don't give a shit about anything else.

Martina's fingers were tight around Greta's. Holding hands again, after all this time.

Mirko and the other two were talking quietly. Then Luca came over to where the two little girls were sitting and told them to get ready because they were going to see something new, something that they couldn't possibly have imagined.

They all sat in a circle on the mattress. Mirko opened his backpack slowly, his big, somewhat clumsy, hands struggling with the cord, yanking at the buckle. He plunged his arm in and pulled out a stack of magazines that rustled in his hands. At first glance they looked like comic books. They laid the magazines down in a row, one next to the other, in the centre of the mattress, in the middle of their circle.

On the first cover: a girl done up like a doll in pink boots, her bra straining over tits as big as melons, her thumbs tucked into the straps, her mouth parted slightly revealing straight teeth, glistening with saliva.

Mirko didn't do anything, he let Luca open the magazine. He had lit a cigarette and, with an amused smile, looked directly at Luca. It was different now, with the girls there. It wasn't like before, when the boys were alone, each one touching himself. Mirko got a kick out of watching Luca's floundering expression. He pushed him.

'You're the teacher, open it up. Explain . . . Show them the pictures.'

'Yeah . . . right . . . just a minute . . .'

Luca passed a hand over his cropped head, pulled his shirt away from his neck with his thumb and index finger. He was sweating; it was almost hard to breathe. Greta and Martina sat in silence, holding hands, waiting. Every now and then they'd look at each other and Greta would let out a sharp, short sound, almost a laugh. She tightened her grip on Martina's hand and pulled her skirt down lower over her thighs with her other hand. Matteo sat still, his hands resting on his knees. Every two seconds, he'd tear his eyes from the pictures to look at Martina.

The magazine was shiny, its pages large and brightly coloured. There were men and women. Naked. The women had triangles between their legs, neatly covered with hair. Below the hair, they opened up like fruit cut in two, split. The men all had really big, erect penises which they pushed into the women's openings. Martina had never seen the kinds of expressions they had on their faces. But there was a familiar wet tremble between her legs, a shiver, that she had been feeling at night in her bed for a long time, her books and dolls around her – she didn't know what it was. A sweet shiver. Powerful. Fast. All she had to do was pass her fingers over that little place, quickly, and it exploded.

What did that have to do with this? The bodies in the magazines were bodies doing strange things together, contorting into incredible positions, like the steps in a gymnastics routine. There wasn't the silence, the solitude, it seemed meaningless. They were pretty to look at, like living sculptures; but they were gross, too. The sweat was damp on their skin, their saliva made glistening foamy trails in their open mouths. It gave you goose pimples and a nasty, sweaty feeling.

Martina got off the bed and crossed over to the table, rested her hands on the rough surface, and slid her fingers over the raised grain of the wood, lightly, so she wouldn't get a splinter.

One of the magazines was spread out on the table, open at the centrefold, but she kept her eyes on the edge of the page. She was waiting for something to happen, for someone to say something, but they were all quiet and the silence coming in from outside, from the fields, scared her too.

Mirko came over to her. He made a few turns, performed a pirouetting kind of dance. Slowly, he stretched out his arms to touch Martina's shoulders with the tips of his fingers. Her eyes glued to the picture on the table – a shapely blonde holding her tits in her hands and staring right into the lens – Martina didn't move. She gave a quick smile with the corner of her mouth and then listened to Mirko's breath drawing closer and closer to her neck. His eyes were fixed on the centrefold, too, and his hands gripped her shoulders, tight. Martina thought it was lovely – lovely, his breath so near, his hands, hot and damp, through the thin fabric of her shirt.

The other two boys had stretched out on the mattresses and were smoking a cigarette while flipping through other magazines. These were all like the first. They didn't talk to each other, they didn't look at each other, they just watched out of the corner of their eyes for a gesture, a flick of a hand, a sign that it was time to turn the page. Lying on their stomachs, waving their legs, their big trainers in the air. Matteo took the cigarette and balanced it on his lips, barely inhaling, his eyes wide open. Luca turned the pages slowly, one at a time.

A woman, legs parted, stretched out on a beach, blue eyes turned to the camera, a fake smile, her skin tanned and gleaming with suntan oil. She was completely shaved, her skin smooth and greasy. Another woman, on her knees, her hands planted on the ground, her arse up in the air, her blue jeans unfastened, revealing a brown triangle, her breasts pointy, pale.

Matteo looked through the smoke, his eyes glued to the page, his heart pounding. He had noticed what was going on between Mirko and Martina across the room, but didn't completely understand. He would have had to turn around

38

and look directly to see Mirko's arm moving, his hand deep in his trousers. But he couldn't. It wasn't the moment. And it wasn't up to him, or even Luca, to decide.

Greta sat on the edge of the bed, nodding her head, singing a song, chewing patiently, precisely, on the nail of her left index finger. Her eyes were blank and fixed on the corner of the decrepit table in front of her.

At first Martina barely noticed the movement: the simple swing of Mirko's hand, an insignificant imperceptible gesture. Then she looked more carefully, purposefully, and saw. She turned her head toward Mirko and drew her gaze down to the farthest corner of her eyeballs, so far it hurt. Mirko's left hand was resting on her shoulder, his right hand was in his trousers, tight around something, a flash of flesh, pink, protruding. He moved it slowly, back and forth; the tip of the thing brushed against her left buttock.

She didn't say anything. She stood still, hands gripping the edge of the table, splinters digging into her palms, arms taut, aching from the strain.

Greta just sat there, her index finger in her mouth, her eyes fixed on the corner of the table.

At this point, Luca got up off the bed, brushing the dust from his shirt. He walked over to Greta in his gangsta-rap way, dragging his feet in their fluorescent green trainers.

It happened quickly. He knelt down in front of Greta, took her face between his hands, brought his mouth to hers and stuck his entire tongue out the moment their lips touched. She tried to turn her head away, murmured something, pushed her hands against his shoulders, but he leaned his face deeper into her. So she stopped, sat still with her mouth open, receiving the hard, pointy tongue, going in and out, scraping against her teeth.

Luca unzipped his trousers and stuck his hand into his boxers. He kept on like that for a little while, then he pulled back from Greta, his eyes half-shut, and, still on his knees, moved his hand back and forth. One hand still tight on the sharp knee of the little girl, who watched him quietly, mute.

On the way back home Martina sat on Mirko's scooter, hanging on to him, with the unpleasant feeling that some-how she had lost something, forgotten something, and that she couldn't do anything about it. All that countryside around them, and something forgotten, or lost.

That was the first time. The first time they went to the shed. The start of this thing between them, this thing that was about them – together. No outsiders looking in.

6

Martina and Greta didn't talk the next day at school. They had Italian for the first two hours; the teacher read out the homework essays from the week before.

The walls and windows of the school were plastered with papers and drawings. From outside, in the grey days of winter, the school was an explosion of garish colour. In their classroom, an enormous, slightly faded map of Europe hung above the teacher's head. After much discussion among themselves and with the teacher, the students had drawn red circles around all the places they had ever been, whispering to each other: Give me the marker . . . I already said that. There were quite a few little circles scattered over Europe. Someone suggested suspiciously that many of the places had only been visited in dreams.

Martina kept her eyes fixed just over the teacher's head, on the map covered with red circles, trying to remember the names of Europe's capital cities in alphabetical order.

Martina liked Italian most of all. She liked history, too, but she liked Italian best. She was top of the class, even in grammar, but her strongest subject was reading comprehension. Martina read a lot of books; her classmates didn't

– not even Greta. Greta still liked picture books for children, or comic books. But even those were hard for her. She rushed through the pages, looking for the illustrations. Once Martina had tried to get her to read something. She lent Greta a book she had just finished, one with an attractive cover: two funny-looking children, identical twins – exactly the same, except that the girl was really tall and skinny and the boy was short. Both of them wore huge black and white striped sweaters. The girl's sweater went all the way down to her knees and the boy's covered half his face. They were running and holding a giant spoon, the Meteorite Spoon. A volcano exploded behind them. Martina thought the book was easy enough and fun – those two ridiculous twins and their parents who never stopped fighting, Mr and Mrs Thunder.

Greta kept the book for two months and, when Martina asked for it back, she didn't remember ever having borrowed it. It was still in her desk at school, hidden under a pile of photocopies and maths exercises.

Through the whole Italian class, while the teacher read essays and talked about syntax, Martina and Greta sat still, their hands on their desks, symmetrical, heads up, their eyes set on the teacher's mouth or over her head. But it was obvious they weren't listening.

One of the classroom windows was open, letting in the chirping of the birds and the rumble of cars and trucks on the main road that ran past the school. The fresh April air, already pregnant with new smells.

The branch of a giant elm tree tapped endlessly against the window frame. Out of the corner of her eye, without moving her head, Martina watched the branch sway, stretch out like an arm and then snap back, elastic. The leaves trembled, shook, convulsed. This image, this fragment of an image, turned her stomach. She didn't know why. It had something to do with Greta's hands resting on her desk, her filed nails with their chipped, dark-red nail varnish. Greta's hands shook too, a barely noticeable tremble, as if some bottled-up violence was about to explode from within her. The muscles of her thin arms were taut. Martina had the impression that they were going to escape, break free, elastic, uncontrolled, like the elm branch.

That afternoon, Martina went into her room after lunch and stretched out on her bed, falling into a sweaty half-sleep full of thoughts. Memories, more than anything else. She was thinking about what had happened the day before, in the shed, of Mirko's hands on her shoulders, the movement in his trousers. She could see Luca, his tongue cramming into Greta's mouth. She thought of that strange, but familiar sensation between her legs when they were looking at the pictures in the magazines. And she thought about something else, too, something that she recalled only in a confused way: a memory of light and smells. A green light, the whole room is green, the green of the floor of the small gymnasium at nursery school, the green of the curtains and walls. Narrow, intense beams of afternoon sun filtering in through the drawn blinds. The children's cots, lined up, one next to the other, for the afternoon rest. So many bodies laid out. The calm breathing, the smell of rubber from the plimsolls everyone wore. One of the teachers sits on a stool near the partly closed door. And Martina lies on her cot,

43

wrapped up in the sheets, her hand on her secret place, racing toward the powerful tremble that, behind her closed eyes, is a meadow, a long path through the dark, in the snow, under the stars, and black horses bucking in their stalls. Black horses – who knows why.

The teacher notices, shuffles across the darkened gymnasium in her orthopaedic shoes, comes to a stop in front of Martina's cot – a massive black shadow – scolds her in a whisper, an angry whisper, waving her hands. She says Martina shouldn't be doing that thing.

There are horses running through the snow, the stars above. There's a leap into emptiness, like rounding a hill at full speed in a car, coming back down so fast your stomach lurches, like getting into a bathtub where the hot water makes you shiver with its intensity – a long shiver, that goes through your whole body, into your bones.

Why shouldn't she do it if it's nice?

Then she remembered the underwear game. They'd play it a lot at school. In the girls' toilet at break, safe from the indiscreet eyes of caretakers and teachers, they'd gather in a circle to Look At Underwear.

It worked like this: each girl in turn would go into the middle of the circle and lift her skirt or pull down her trousers to show the others her knickers. There were boys there, too, the ones who had managed to slip into the toilet without being seen. It was all about negotiation, upping the ante, like at an auction. You'd show your underwear and in exchange someone would have to let you copy the maths homework or give you a chocolate bar for two days running.

The boys didn't show their pants. Maybe they did,

among themselves in the boys' toilet where the girls never went. But not there; it was always a girl who showed herself off. Usually, it was one of the plain ones. The girls who seemed already more grown up. Country girls, the fat, clumsy ones who wore braces on their teeth and dressed like Easter eggs.

Greta and Martina never played those stupid games. But they watched sometimes, dragged along to the toilet by some friend, sucked into the frenetic circle that pressed in tightly around the Underwear Show, like at a concert or stadium.

So, on those rare occasions, they had seen.

Martina thinks of Mara, from 4–B. Mara is very plain and when she says 'S', her spongy, wet tongue sticks out over her teeth. Under her green velour dress decorated with red deer, her huge knickers were the colour of putty, or bread dough and coming apart at the seams. Round and soft, with a kind of yellowish halo in the middle. Had Mara peed herself?

Greta was different. Martina had thought about this the day before, when Greta climbed on to Luca's scooter, lifting her leg so that a bit of underwear with a lace border peeped out from under her short skirt. She had remembered Mara from 4–B, in the girls' toilet, pulling up her skirt to show off her underwear to half the school, a blank expression on her face. The two things were totally different, but something mysterious tied them together. Secrets linked, for sure, to the way that Chiara, in their class, would sometimes curl her foot up on to her seat under her bottom. In the middle of the lesson, she'd swing her other foot back and forth, maintaining an stony expression as she moved.

Martina fell asleep to the noise of the crickets outside in the field, the sun beating into the corner of her room, coming to rest on the bookshelf. On the red spine of *Pippi Longstocking*, one of her mother's old books.

Deep in sleep, her thoughts melted into her dreams.

7

The next time, and the times after that, everything went more quickly and more slowly. More quickly, in the sense that the moment Martina saw Mirko arrive on his scooter, heading over to Luca and Matteo, she got ready to jump on the back of his seat. Greta, too, stopped asking questions. She let herself fall in with the will of the others, trailing the group in silence.

More slowly, because it all lasted for such a long time. The afternoons stretched out, full of details, movements, puzzles.

They all had more or less the same curfew, but they'd completely forget about it until a quarter of an hour before. Their place was a place apart, different, with its own laws. A place where the gaze, the authority, the love too, of mothers and fathers never entered. From the moment they climbed on to their scooters and crossed the fields, the rest of their lives disappeared. School had nothing to do with it, and neither did their courtyard games; it all evaporated – as did their other friends, and the people they themselves had been until only a short time before. Even age vanished. They were small, little children and big, grown-up children at the same time. Their only subjects of discussion were what was happening there in the shed or the games they had played together when they were little.

Relationships between them were defined yet fluid. Mirko was the leader, then came Luca. No one dreamed of questioning that. It was right. Things became less organised when they were all naked, united and equal in front of each other. Their bodies were similar. Sure, male and female were different, but only in one respect. Otherwise, they all had flat, smooth stomachs and narrow hips; taut, unblemished, hairless skin. And they moved without grace, dangling their arms and legs – not yet fully in control of them.

One day Mirko said that each of them had to bring one thing to the shed – not just anything, something important, something meaningful. They should bring in their most prized possession, what they cared about most, that way the shed would become somewhere special to go to, a place that was part of them, like their rooms at home.

But, they had to remember that, once they brought their contribution to the shed, it would belong to everyone and they couldn't take it back. And they shouldn't even consider putting one over on him, because Mirko would be able to tell if they'd brought something they didn't really care about.

Luca brought his gameboy. The little monitor had become almost a part of him from the moment he'd got it as a present. He took it everywhere he went, even to school, holding it on his knee under the desk, hidden by a strategically placed pile of books, beating his own record –

no one ever caught on. He cheered in silence while he and Super Mario leapt like cheetahs over unbelievable obstacles, landing safe and sound on the other side of an ocean. He told his parents that it had been stolen. Now it lay on the bed in the shed, amid the pillows and rumpled covers. They held massive gameboy tournaments, fighting like animals over the scores which they kept records of in a notebook.

He also brought his favourite tennis racket. It had purple strings and green tape wrapped around the handle. It was old, and he didn't really use it any more, but he cared about it a lot. It had been his first racket; he'd won the summer school tournament with it and it gave him a little callus on the palm of his right hand, at the base of his middle finger.

Martina brought in two things too. A huge drawing she'd done in the second year of her cat, Nero (now long dead), poking his head out of a luxuriant bush, his green eyes open wide and his fur ruffled around his long whiskers, a blue sky behind enormous red and orange tropical flowers. They hung it on the only wall that got light from the window and it looked great hanging there. She also brought a pink ceramic mug. It was very big, with a fat, round handle. She told her mother she had broken it and thrown away the pieces because they were too small to glue back together. Now they'd fill it with chocolate, fanta, or iced tea and all drink from it, passing it around the circle, turning it in their hands, trying to find a dry spot for their lips.

Matteo brought an illuminated globe that ran on batteries. When they closed the door, they'd turn it on and the orange light lit up the whole room. They could see the reliefs of mountains and the delicate tracks of rivers, the bodies of water wrapped around the continents and the green earth, stretched out across the great plains. It was like travelling, like being everywhere.

Mirko counted his thing as the ghetto blaster he'd already brought. He didn't really have anything he cared about, but the others didn't know that. He didn't have precious objects, nothing that represented him or that he loved. He had always been like that, even when he was little: things turned to dust in his hands within hours. He broke everything and never regretted it. He just thought a ghetto blaster would be useful. Music would be good in there.

Greta had chosen to bring a little, fat cactus plant, with a single yellow flower that was already slightly withered. They put it on the table and would sometimes accidentally brush against it and then curse because the needles stuck in their skin and it hurt like hell to get them out.

There weren't many things, but it was a start. Little by little, as the days passed, these objects became familiar parts of their geography. Until they almost didn't notice them, they were so used to having them there, to navigating around them. Coming to the shed was like coming home and recognising the colours, proportions and placement of objects and furniture – so that, even in the dark, they'd know how to find them with the tip of a finger, how to keep from banging their knees into things.

8

It was the girls' turn to lead the game that afternoon, though it was Mirko who set the rules. He gave orders with concentration, curt gestures, a nod of his head. One hand rested on Luca's shoulder as if Mirko was a general, and Luca his second in command.

They all sat on the mattress eating juicy white peaches big as melons. The juice dripped down their fingers and on to their legs; it slid down their chins, their necks; it fell on the covers making sticky puddles. They wiped their fingers on the bed, roughly, and laughed. They would never be allowed to eat like this at home – not giving a shit if the place was a pigsty.

Greta went outside to fill the metal bucket with water from the pump. The water made a happy sound against the sides of the bucket, like falling coins. With their faces and fingers sticky with peach juice, they all ran outside to the pump, laughing and shoving each other as they went.

Mirko stood apart, the usual cigarette in his hand, a smile on his face. The two little girls decided that Matteo would be their first victim. He didn't protest and let himself be dragged along, tripping over brushwood. He stood still, squinting in the strong afternoon light while they stripped him of his shirt and trousers, letting him keep his underwear and shoes on. The upper half of his slender body was tanned: his stomach and arms, and his calves, too – all the colour of honey. But his thighs were chalk white, and his nipples were little stains, lipstick kisses.

The two girls pranced around him, laughing and shouting in the icy spray. They soaped him all over and then rinsed him off, running the water from the pump at full strength. He smiled at the contact of their smooth hands and the cool water.

The tape player, resting on the ground and melting in the heat, blasted out Soundgarden at top volume. Seen through squinted eyes, paralysed by the reverb, the sun really did turn black.

They dried him off slowly after his bath, making him raise his arms and spread his legs so they could get to all the hidden nooks and crannies. Then they sat him on a stool and pulled out the scissors. His soft blond hair fell away from the blades in tight, wet curls. His neck seemed even thinner now. They passed an electric razor, stolen from Paolo, over his head, shaving him clean. His scalp was so pale it seemed blue. There was a tiny cut on the back of his neck and a drop of bright, shiny blood sprang out of it, seeming extra red against the white of his skin.

The sight of him made them laugh – but not to hurt his feelings. They all laughed, singing along to Black Hole Sun and clapping their hands. Matteo kept his head lowered, his prominent vertebrae making bumps over his long neck. What was his mother going to say when she saw him.

★

Later, inside the shed, Martina wrapped her lips around Matteo's penis. It was different from Mirko's. Small, tender, like a finger without any bones. Spongy. Dry. She caressed it with the tip of her tongue, like Mirko had taught her. It only grew a little, but it did get harder. A pink finger. Matteo kept his eyes shut, his hands gripping and releasing the sheets. His thighs trembled and his eyebrows were raised in two dramatic arches. His mouth was open. At a certain point, he let out a little cry – sharp and short. Martina lifted her head to look at his face, pulling her lips off him. She put a finger on her tongue and looked into his eyes with an intensely serious expression.

'Why didn't you make wet?'

'I don't know . . . Wet what? What do you mean?'

Martina shrugged her shoulders and didn't answer. Instead she went over to put in another Soundgarden tape. She wanted to hear that really sad song where they talk about life being like a suicide.

Matteo stayed curled up on the mattress in silence. He was still shivering. Even though it was murderously hot inside the shed, the sun beating down on the tin roof, making it steam, the air still and thick, he felt chilled to the bone. A horrible cold, in the core of his heart. This must be how grown-ups feel, he thought. That was why his mother cried at night.

The first time Martina took Mirko in her hand, a peculiar sensation came over her. His thing – soft and hard at the same time, sticky and hot – was strange to her, but familiar, as if she already knew all about it, as if she'd met it before but forgotten. She immediately started moving her hand back and forth over the loose skin, easily, without thinking about it. As if it were hers, some part of her body she'd been neglecting. Weird. This knowledge that came from within.

A lot of things seemed to happen in this way – coming out of a deep, dark place. Things you didn't know you had inside of you, but that came out when they had a reason to.

It was the same for Matteo, kneeling between the little girls' open legs to look at It close up.

At first he was disappointed. It was so different from what he'd imagined – and the photographs gave a totally different impression. The mysterious architecture of flesh, opening and closing – its hidden holes and valleys, curves and swellings, its layers – was monstrous from close up. But then Mirko lifted his heavy hand from where it was resting inert on the mattress and told him to stick his finger into the central opening. He moved his finger in and out, and then from side to side, feeling the hot, wet flesh wrap around him, suck at him. It was the same sensation as when he put his finger in his mouth to lick up cake dough left over in the bowl.

He too thought that this was something strange – something he already knew.

It was the same every time. There was the sensation of novelty, followed by strangeness, repeating itself with every new gesture, everything they learned in those days.

And there was confusion, too. Like when someone comes over to visit and touches all your things, moves your books, listens to your records, sits on your bed, looks out your window – and there you are after they've left, alone in your room with the lingering smell of other people's bodies, traces of their presence, heavy in the air. Bodies aren't like rooms. People passing through bodies don't leave visible clues. But it's still the same: even if there are no bruises, or wounds, there's still the smell of sweat, the imprint of kisses, swollen genitals. Even when there's nothing you can see, there's still confusion. On the inside.

They all experienced these sensations unquestioningly in their afternoons together at the shed. Strangeness, newness, familiarity, and confusion – all elements of the same substance. A fluid, rubbery substance that spread over their insides, making them feel mushy and thick.

The boys didn't do anything to each other. They'd watch, make silent comparisons, but never comment. They shared the girls equally, exchanging, one after the other. They looked and touched. Sometimes they laughed. Sometimes they teased – vulgar boy jokes, following a code that excluded the girls.

There was no caressing, especially at the beginning. They were playing a game with pre-established rules and, anyway, no one wanted too much soppiness. If, by accident, they came too close with their lips, they'd pull back and wipe their faces with the back of their hand – as if they had been kissed by the slimy, greedy mouths of relatives or something.

It all smelled different to what they expected. Their sweat smelled of salty lemon juice, or of ripe, sticky plums. It was the perfume of a little animal, the fur of a wet dog or a long-haired cat. The combination of sweet and salty gave them shivers, clung to their tongues. It was all so different from the way their mothers smelled – the smell of grown-ups in general. It was a wild smell, mixed with the sweetness of soap or shampoo: apple shampoo and the sourness of milk stains round their mouths.

Even their skin felt different from what they'd imagined. It was soft and dry as paper in some places, and rough in others. In other places it was slippery and slimy. And they didn't all feel the same to the touch. Each one of them had their own particular consistency, their own particular balance of perfume and stink. One of their games was to close their eyes and try to identify each other with the tips of their tongues, licking and sucking like a litter of kittens.

Then they would knock each other on to the mattress and roll around with their eyes still closed, laughing like crazy at their stupid, beautiful game.

Mirko was the only one who didn't join in. The silly games disgusted him. His body was too easy to identify anyway. He already had tufts of hair under his armpits and a long narrow strip of hair running down his belly. Sometimes his smell was too strong, almost like an adult's – recognisable. He'd let them frolic on the bed, but wouldn't watch. It was as if he were absent. The others were so obviously children and he felt as if he'd already moved beyond them, that he was too old for such things. He'd have liked to escape, get out of the shed, be fifteen again, and doing things other fifteen-year-olds did. But he stayed, waited for them to finish the bullshit so they could get back to playing the way he wanted to.

9

Two girls were watching Matteo from behind the goal at the end of the football field and he was sure he'd seen them before. He'd glance over at them out of the corner of his eye in between passing the ball. The blonde looked a little like Paolo's girlfriend, who had long legs and was always wearing short socks and miniskirts to show them off. She had to be over twenty. The other girl looked like a child – fifteen, maybe – but she was probably older than twenty, too. Drops of sweat fell into his eyes.

It wasn't a great game, and Matteo wasn't very good at football anyway. His mother had forced him into it. He would rather have done swimming. The cool, pool water in his ears. Silence and the slap of artificial waves against the cement walls. Blue water, blue tiles on the bottom. His legs and arms beating rhythmically down a straight line – his eyes open to keep on course. His body hugged, held up by the water. But his mother had insisted on football because it was a team sport and he needed to be with other boys. He was too short for basketball, so football it was.

Even though he ran slowly, he was sweating. His head was spinning and his feet slipped on the squashed grass, as if the field were moving by itself, a conveyor belt, rolling to a completely different rhythm from the pounding of his feet. The games they had played the day before at the shed had worn out his legs. His knees felt like jelly.

Why were those two girls still standing at the net? What could be so intriguing about junior league football practice?

He ran unevenly, his head hanging to one side. It was really hot. Sweat dripped into his T-shirt, his shorts. Dripped down into his shoes, soaking his socks. With a flash of his arms, while running, he pulled his T-shirt over his head and threw it to the ground at the corner of the field. It was his favourite red shirt and the number 19 patch sewn on to it matched his cap. Balled up and heavy with sweat, it landed near where the two girls stood watching. They smiled – or, at least, he thought they smiled. He glanced down quickly at his chest and saw his muscles, firm and shiny. He was so much smaller than the others, he was still too thin and smooth all over. Not a hair. Slender, pale. You could see the blue tracks of his veins crossing the surface of his transparent skin. They looked like streams of water: little rivers and their estuaries.

The girls were still there when the game was over; it seemed like they were looking right at him. Every so often, they'd laugh and then make some comment. He couldn't imagine what they were saying to each other.

His heart pounding, he took a shower and packed his bag. It was time to leave. He was going to have to cross the gravel road circling the field to get to his bicycle which he'd left leaning up against the fence, less then a metre from where the girls were standing. They watched him. He walked slowly, his backpack slung over one shoulder, eyes down, his baseball cap low over his face. His skinny legs poked out of his baggy blue jeans, cut off halfway down his calves.

What were they still doing there? He was the last one out of the dressing room. Everyone else was already in the car park in front of the field: the older kids on their scooters, the others with their bikes. Some of the boys were being picked up by their mothers.

Their looks embarrassed him. He could feel the red crawling up his cheeks. It was as if they were standing there inside the shed, watching him laid out on the mattress, watching Mirko touch Greta with the tip of his tongue, licking her up her thighs, higher, pushing her knickers aside.

He always blushed.

He still hadn't done much at the shed, but even just looking is an experience. There's no going back once you've seen it. You grow up, you learn things.

Smiling and winking at each other the girls watched him walk towards them, waved, then turned back to the field to wave at the coach. It was him they had been waiting for – obviously.

Matteo pushed his bike all the way home, letting the pedals knock hard against his shin. He could already picture the blue bruise that he was going to get. And could see his mother kneeling down on one leg to spread lanolin over it, her hair dried out by the lemon juice she used to make it lighter and by the straightening comb. His mother's hair had an acidic smell. Martina's hair smelled different. Maybe his mother smelled more like a woman: strong and a little acidic.

He had watched the girls disappear down the road with his coach. He thought about his bruise and how women smelled. Too many things at once: smells, the shed, the games. He was tired. He climbed the stairs to where his mother was waiting. She would have his dinner ready, and would watch him eat – like she always did – then she'd sit in front of the TV and come over every now and then to check his homework. She'd stand looking over his shoulder, maybe she'd run her fingers through his hair, flip the pages of his open book. After homework, bed. He had a small bed, a child's bed, fresh white and blue sheets, tucked tightly under the mattress. His pyjama bottoms were short and had little boats on them. It was nice to sleep, in the dark, the boats sailing lightly over him, his tired leg muscles finally relaxing, his mother sitting next to him, her hand in his hair – as she did every evening, for a little while. She was all alone, so she was a little sad. That's why she'd started checking up on him before going to sleep. She sat on the corner of his little-boy bed, put her hand in his hair, her eyes bright in the dark. Then she slipped away, just a shadow, hardly darker than the other shadows.

After he'd heard the bathroom door open and the door of the other bedroom shut with a little click, he'd start his thinking. He'd pull aside the covers and put his hand on the tight, flat muscles of his stomach. His penis sticking out between his legs. A soft little thing, its flesh more tender than the rest of him. It was completely different from the ones in the magazines. It was completely different from Luca's and Mirko's. Perhaps because he was the smallest, or perhaps because he was the youngest.

The first time he'd asked Mirko about it, Mirko had teased him, the tone of his voice, as usual, ironic, nasty. He though about Mirko's nasty answer for days and felt different, offended. He got scared and stopped touching himself. He'd go to bed and put his arms under the pillow so he wouldn't be tempted to explore this thing he didn't understand. The next time he'd asked, Mirko didn't act like an arsehole and told him that he'd get bigger too. That sooner or later the white liquid that the magazine guys sprayed all over the women's faces would come out of his little hole. It would probably happen at night, while he was sleeping, from rubbing his legs together, or rubbing himself against his sheets. That's how it usually happened. For now, nothing. He'd touch himself there and feel something incomprehensible, something nice that he associated with Martina and the two girls watching him play football, and the bodies of the naked women in the magazines. Still nothing would come out.

After thinking, Matteo would fall fast asleep, his hand resting in that soft pulsating hollow, between his leg and his thing. A drop of saliva slid off his lip, his perspiration evaporated as his body slowed into sleep. The boats sailed back and forth for a little while longer, then stopped.

They came to get him at football practice one day. Matteo was running slowly. They could just make him out in the confusion of boys – all of them taller and larger than Matteo, and more worked up. The team divided into two groups for practice. The only way you could tell the groups apart was by the colour of their socks: blue or yellow. They all wore different shirts. The field stretched out endlessly between the goal posts, much too big to be running across for all that time.

Mirko and Luca stood against the wire fence, their fingers gripping it like talons, swinging off it, making the whole thing sway.

The moon was in the middle of the sky, directly over the field – plump and round, still pale in the violent blue sky.

They got fed up standing around waiting for him. Then the bastard coach, for some reason, made him do two extra laps around the field. All the other boys ran about, practising big kicks. Matteo ran slowly, his eyes lowered, glued to the ground.

While they were walking back down the town's main street – a suffocating heat rising up off the asphalt, the air wavering between the cars in the distance – they started to talk. Matteo walked his bike, the way he always did after practice because his leg muscles were too sore to work the pedals. Mirko and Luca followed close behind, kicking the stones along the edge of the road, making them spin out against the wheels of the passing cars.

Mirko started it by asking Matteo if he had any clue at all about sex. He wanted to know if Matteo knew, in concrete terms, what screwing was. Matteo looked out over the fast cars at the television masts in the middle of the fields and didn't answer. So Luca launched into an eccentric but believable explanation.

'It's basically like kissing someone. Get it?'

Matteo nodded in agreement, his eyes still glued to the road, his hands welded to the handlebars.

'You keep your tongue stiff, straight and you push it into

the girl's mouth. It's the same with sex, except instead of your tongue you use your dick . . . Right?'

'And you have to move your hips back and forth . . . and side to side.'

Matteo took off his cap and wiped his hand over his shaved head, damp with sweat. Then he came to a sudden stop and looked right at Luca. There was a lot of traffic on the road. Everyone coming home from the office, crammed into their cars, arms dangling out of the windows in search of a breath of air. The lucky ones were sealed inside cool, air-conditioned cocoons, their faces blank, the stereos cranked, surrounded by the smell of vanilla air-freshener or mentholated pine.

'Yeah. I get it. I already knew that, pretty much . . . But, what does it have to do with me anyway? I have to go home now . . . Okay? I have to go.'

There was always something that eluded Matteo in the vague and rather idiotic things that Luca said. And then someone was always telling him to do something: his mother made him do football, his teacher made him do his homework, his coach with those extra laps around the field. Now even his friends . . .

'I have to go. Really.'

Mirko nodded yes and so did Luca – a dismissal. They walked him to the gate of his house. It was a little pistachio-coloured house, with a dark wooden door, so little and round it seemed like it was right out of *Snow White and the Seven Dwarfs*.

'Are you still coming to the lime pit tonight? We're only going for a couple of hours after dinner, on our bikes. Ask your mother, now. She's out on the balcony. Come on.'

Luca looked at him, tilting his head just a little to the left, his eyes squinting into the last rays of the sun, low over the field, shining right in his face. His little potato nose wrinkled up.

'I don't need to ask right now. It's Saturday, anyway. I can go out for a while. Come and get me at eight thirty.'

'Affirmative. Eight thirty. Here. On bikes. Everyone on bikes, no scooters.'

He watched them walk away across the island of dry grass and dusty mud in the middle of the road, hands deep in their pockets, kicking stones as they went. Mirko was a little taller than Luca. From behind he looked like a tree with messed up leaves, beaten by the wind. A tall, straight, dried-up tree. Or a broken-down lamp post.

10

They usually went to the lime pit during the day. When it was light, it was just a square filled with brown water. In the dark it turned into a lake. The water seemed bright blue and reflected the trees: a tiara of branches floating over the water's smooth surface. The moon was a white plate, empty, in the middle of the still water. The bells of the church rang on the quarter-hour.

Greta and Martina were walking around the rim of the pit, their shoes sinking dangerously into the damp earth that gave way under their weight. They walked close, but didn't touch. They talked in a whisper, so the boys wouldn't hear them, but voices in the country are amplified and float up and out, like dust blown on the wind. Lazing on the ground at the foot of a giant tree, the boys looked up at the stars peeking down through the leaves and could only make out muffled words here and there. They tried to reconstruct the girls' conversation without any luck. It all seemed like stupid nonsense. They listened distractedly. Girls' talk didn't interest them much anyway. They preferred their own company. Sometimes, when it was just boys, it was better to sit in silence, to share space without needing to explain anything.

Mirko had brought some weed and rolled a joint with impressive skill, twisting the paper between his middle finger and thumb, flicking his tongue down the length of it to close it up – as if he had spent the last five years doing nothing else. He passed it to Luca so he could add the paper filter and light it. They let their heads rest on the grass and smoked with their eyes closed.

Matteo sat on a tree stump, his elbows on his knees, his eyes fixed on the two girls walking around the pit. He wasn't listening to them. He was too busy thinking about his own things. He was thinking that he'd rather be walking with the girls around the pit, but he didn't have the guts to get up and join them.

Walking around the pit, under the limpid moonlight, the girls spied a scrap of paper floating on the water's surface. They could just make out faded writing and some drawings. It looked like the remains of a letter, that someone had maybe ripped up and tossed into the pit in order to forget what had been written there.

Greta stood at the edge of the water and leaned out, her shoes sinking into the damp earth and slipping on the wet grass. Martina held on to her arm, anchoring her feet on an embedded rock, and hung her entire body out in the opposite direction. The tips of her fingers were stretching toward a branch to grab the leaves for support, when a rock suddenly came skittling down the bank, flew straight into the water and sank, taking the paper down with it.

They went back to where the others were sitting by the huge tree, a little disappointed at having lost their discovery

– the romantic adventure that might have been revealed in that scrap of letter.

Martina described how once she had found a piece of paper, carefully folded and hidden under the arm rest on a bus. She had grabbed it and tucked it away in her pocket. When she got off the bus, she anxiously opened the letter, hoping it would reveal some great mystery. But it was only notes on how to interpret children's compositions through their drawings and paintings. Perhaps it belonged to a teacher. Martina had kept the piece of paper in between the pages of her notebook. She would imagine the face of the woman who'd written it, sitting at home, leaning over her desk, a light shining on a page of the notebook. There was no one else in the house. Martina imagined the woman's hand curled around a pen, her lowered head, the pressure of the nib crossing the soft paper. Everything that she still had left to write about, all the other pieces of paper covered with the neat, clear calligraphy that teachers have.

No one said anything. Luca kept his eyes closed and let his head loll on the grass.

They listened to the crickets and the sudden little splashes of frogs in the water. They sat together in silence for a while, then someone proposed a game, which led to a big discussion about the rules. It was a word game: Who Knew the Most Bad Words. A silly game to be playing there in the dark at the foot of an enormous tree.

They started a catalogue of dirty words – all the ones they knew. Luca went first and everyone listened attentively, except Mirko who continued to drift, an oblique smile on his face.

'Arse. That's the first one I learned . . . It's the first one you learn.'

'Okay, arse, and then what?'

'Dick, you learn that right away, too.'

'Then all of the ones like shit, crap, pee.'

'Yeah, right. But those aren't even dirty words – in a sense.'

'What sense?'

'Come on, they don't have anything to do with it.'

'So, pussy, and cunt, or beaver.'

'Gross, those are all so ugly. Totally gross.'

Luca and Greta were doing all the talking. Martina was playing with the tip of one of Matteo's shoes. She stuck a little twig in a hole in the stitching, trying to get to his skin and tickle him. Matteo sat quietly, his eyes watching Martina's hand. But she kept looking over at Mirko, shooting him glances every so often, until Mirko realised she was watching him and he caught her gaze and held it.

Luca continued his list of bad words, looking steadily at the girls sitting in front of him. He wrinkled his nose and tilted his head slightly to one side, crunching his neck into his shoulders. A fraction of a smile on one side of his mouth. Hateful. Greta watched him indifferently. She stopped answering him. Martina lowered her eyes. She had a strange feeling in her stomach, a twinge that came every time she looked at Mirko. His face in the shadows was like a quickly drawn sketch: his profile sharp and hard, chiselled; his strange, big mouth, turned down at the corners.

It was then that Mirko said it. Said that thing that no one understood, but that they would all remember for a long time, that they would keep asking themselves the meaning of and why he'd said it there, that evening, by the lime pit. The words came out slowly with long pauses between each one. He seemed very serious as he spoke, his face turned towards the black, glistening water, his expression fixed and unreadable.

'We can't hook up. Don't forget that . . . We can't be like other people, do the whole couple thing . . . hooking up within the group. That's against the rules. And it wouldn't mean anything. We're all in this together, or else, nothing. As long as we don't start getting involved, nothing will ever have to change.'

When they remembered that night spent in the middle of the fields, they'd think that the whole story might have gone in another direction if they had only stayed on the banks of the lime pit, at night, or in the courtyard in the afternoon, coming together gradually, teasing each other, maybe even wrestling before kissing on the lips, quickly, close-mouthed. Their hands tucked deep into their pockets.

11

The soft light in the shed drew out the length of Mirko's eyes, making them seem even narrower, more liquid. His mouth, still closed, slowly touched Martina's.

This kissing stuff always lasted a long time. You moved your lips under the other person's slightly-open mouth – you stroked their neck and hair. It wasn't difficult, like petting a cat, but wetter, and it made your heart race.

She could see Greta watching them in silence from the edge of the mattress, hugging her knees. Greta didn't like to kiss. She had always thought it was disgusting. She never actually said it, but you could tell from the way she turned her head away as soon as she could, the way she wiped her mouth on her bare shoulder to clean off the spit. All the excess of tongue, lips and teeth revolted her. It was dirty and wet. When you get dirty and wet, you clean up and dry off.

Meanwhile, Martina was thinking about Brenda and Dylan, in a convertible by the ocean, REM singing Losing My Religion in the background. No, it wasn't the same. And Brenda had tits, while Martina . . . But Mirko didn't notice. He'd run his fingers over her chest, rubbing non-

71

existent roundness. He moved his hands just like he was squeezing two breasts. Martina thought that this might make them grow: because he felt them and she believed it. That it might make them blossom. Lifting her head slightly, she saw her thin, naked legs, bristling with tiny blonde hairs. She shifted to let his hand in. How could she know if they were doing it right?

The image of two people she had seen one day at the Margherita Gardens in Bologna came into her mind. They had been sitting in front of the pond where there were ducks and these huge goldfish. Her mouth was open over his, her hands hidden under his sweater. Her eyes were open: she was looking into the deep water, not into his eyes. She watched the monstrous fish, their toothless mouths and rotten gills. She concentrated on the mouldy green water, and the expression in her eyes was serious.

And now, looking right into Mirko's eyes, Martina saw the fish floating belly up, dead, their skin faded and blotchy. She told him to get off her, to move. Enough was enough, it was getting late. And the fish kept crowding his eyes, more and more of them, enormous. There were so many they started blocking out the whites of his eyes. She felt a slow rip and then something soft but clinging stirred inside her. So this was love. Dead fish and a painful rip. Four faces standing over her, laughing and teasing, pinching her stretched-out thighs. Their long arms and hands like talons.

Luca and Matteo were kneeling at the side of the bed. Their trousers were undone and they were holding themselves in their hands. It's a game, said Mirko. Like in the magazines. Look. He reached across the mattress and grabbed a tattered magazine from the floor. There was an Asian girl on the cover. Her hair was shiny, like a doll, and it hung down over her breasts. Three men gathered around her, each in a different position. One stood behind her, his hands tight on her hips, his groin against her arse. Another was in front of her and held his hand between her legs. The other was on his knees, his arms on the ground. The heel of her boot dug into his spine.

Big red letters said GANG BANG.

Martina didn't understand. But what was there to understand? They were bodies that played together, and she just had to ignore stuff like the painful rip or the dead fish – stuff that didn't really have anything to do with her and Mirko, the magazines, the shed. Childish stuff.

Mirko started moving more quickly over her and the others watched. Greta, too, had now entered her field of vision. Greta was only wearing her lace knickers – nothing else. Her body was slim and white. There were two pale, pointy roses on her chest, just budding. She wasn't smiling her Smile, but her eyes were calm – at least, Martina thought they were. And if Greta was calm, then she, too, could be. She could close her eyes, listen to all the breathing, mixed up, around her. Wait for the pain to go away.

Later, when she got up off the mattress, she realised there was blood coming out of her, not a lot, but she was frightened. She didn't say anything, but stood with her hand pressed between her legs.

Mirko handed her a kleenex and she understood from the neutral expression on his face that it was normal. Blood was okay, it was supposed to be there. So she didn't make any comment. She pulled her knickers back on and then her jumper. She laced up her boots without looking up, pretending that everything was as it should be, that nothing was wrong.

Greta's first time came a few days later. But it wasn't with Mirko. With a magnanimous wave of his hand, and few words, he let it be understood that Luca would take her. He turned her over to him after she was already spread out on the bed, her skirt pulled up around her belly. It was Luca's first time too. No one knew about Mirko. He had never said anything about it. But once, when Mirko wasn't there, Luca had repeated this incredible story, insinuating that Mirko did it all the time.

Mirko didn't tell Luca anything, he just gestured cavalierly and shot him a sarcastic look. As if to say, welcome to the amazing, grown-up world of fucking. Luca tried to stall, he half undressed, then he gulped down some orange soda, put a tape on and sat down on the bed near Greta.

Matteo and Martina were playing with the gameboy and didn't look up from the screen. Greta lay immobile on the bed, her eyes closed and her fingers clutching the rolled hem of her skirt. Her legs were closed tightly together.

Luca raised his hand along with the explosion of drum and bass from the tape. You got to raise up sweet woman child, said the singer in an angry voice.

Greta opened her eyes but her expression stayed the same. Luca's hand rested on her closed knees, his mouth was parted and near hers. They looked at each other for a long time, then Luca slid his body over the petrified girl. From where he was sitting at the table, Mirko watched and smiled. Luca's movements were clumsy and inconclusive. He was hurting her. You could tell from the way her eyes squeezed shut and her mouth was curling. Then it happened. What was supposed to happen, happened. Right under everyone's eyes. The same way it had been for Martina.

A lot was lost in those moments. And a lot of new things came – from where, no one knew: emotions, hard and direct, like punches in the face; things you don't forget, empty of sweetness, hard enough to make you cry when you remember them. Things that divided them and united them in an instant. As with everything you do in this world together with somebody else.

12

They often ate together, naked on the mattress. Sandwich wrappers, crumbs from cakes, and drops of melted ice cream on their faces and legs. They'd shop at the supermarket on the main road in town, counting out their coins on the counter in front of the impatient cashier. With their backpacks full of provisions, they'd head up the road to the shed. It was steep and the scooters wobbled as if they were all drunk. They'd hold their helmets under their arms and let their hair blow in the wind.

They alternated between the magazine game and the games they used to play. The old games would come up spontaneously and suddenly they were themselves again – children playing hide-and-seek or red light, green light. The same children who could spend hours talking about what dogs eat, or about the best trainers, or the latest terrifying episode of *The X Files*. They'd run naked through the shed, singing – just like they used to.

Greta's cheeks would go red when she was out of breath – the two pink flowers on her chest rising and falling heavily. Mirko would be the one to restore order. They'd return to the bed, stretch out, and teach each other things.

They'd look at the magazines – there was always something new – and try the positions.

A tongue between Greta's thighs. Everyone together. Or: Martina and Greta stand against each other and we'll watch. Or: You, here, put it here. Rest it on the hole and push it in with your hand.

Sometimes it would just make them laugh. Then they'd argue about some detail, and keep on like that until they were all exhausted.

Martina had taught Mirko how to touch that place the way she liked it. She explained it to him precisely, as if she were teaching him how to work the controls of a video game.

Put your finger in this position, keep it pressed like that, and now move it slowly.

It was strange to teach someone else about your own body. They had never thought about the exact terminology for things. The mechanisms were simple – response to stimulation. The instinctive movements they'd always known about. Movements without names. But now that they were explaining things to each other, they had to construct sentences and so everything took on a new meaning.

Martina thought about her body, about this thing she had lived in all by herself for so long, and was now sharing with other people. She taught Mirko what paths to follow in order to reach the right places. She knew where they were. And she learned. She learned things about herself, things about other bodies, how they were different, how they were the same, and how their bodies fitted into hers.

She felt pain sometimes, or disgust – but in the end, that's all it was.

Good and bad, like at school, like at home, like everywhere.

Suddenly, something changed. And from something, everything. They began to get bored. It had lasted too long. It was like with the rollerblading. For a while they had done nothing but rollerblade from morning to night, until they were sick of it. Then the rollerblades disappeared and no one talked about them any more. So they started a new game, with new possibilities.

For a few days they didn't even go to the shed. When they met in the courtyard, they'd be shy – almost as if they were disgusted with each other. They'd chat in embarrassment about this and that. They all knew it was time to take a break. Time to think about school again, about homework, about their families, time to play with their dogs, to watch TV and torture the cat, time to get bored on their own. Their afternoons together had turned into an obligation, like homework. They were mostly just a trial.

Ten days passed. It was June and there were things to wrap up before school finished for the summer. They were all busy cramming for save-your-arse final exams. An onslaught of schoolwork, teachers, families.

And then there was the class portrait ritual. Greta and Martina, 5-F, Academic Year 1995–96. The two girls stand apart – one on each side of the picture. Martina looks directly into the lens, without smiling. Her hands are tucked into the pockets of her red overalls, and her hair is covering her mouth. Greta has been distracted and is looking down at the ground, maybe at something that she

79

dropped. She is about to bend over and get it.

The photographer snapped the picture at the very moment in which Greta decided to lean over. Her thin body is caught as it bends. She seems on the point of shooting out of the photo, a violent and stiff twist of her waist, frozen on the film.

13

The day after school ended they were all together again in the yard. Big kids and little kids. A mass of children: loud, restless. Split up into little, tight-knit groups. Greta and Martina sat together on a bench by themselves talking about their summer plans. Greta was lucky. She was going to the beach on the island of Elba with her cousins and aunts who were all very young and would go dancing every night in this gorgeous club looking out over the water. They'd be with their German friends who also went there every year. Greta had friends, too: the German kids, with their white hair and skin that turned bright red in the sun, who always stuck out their entire tongues to lick their ice-cream cones.

Martina wasn't going anywhere. She always stayed at home through the summer. She used to go away to camp when she was younger. One year she went to the mountains with her church group. Then her family stopped worrying about her summer vacations. Since they couldn't go away, neither would she. Maybe in mid-August she'd go with her mother to visit her aunt in the hills of Ferrara. That meant mosquitoes and humidity, women gossiping under suffocating umbrellas.

Greta talked and talked, happy and smiling. Martina looked at her in silence. She watched her little red lips curl up into her nose. She knew those lips so well, knew how they felt. She watched Greta's hands. Hands that had touched her all over. She looked at Greta's protruding collarbone. Martina's own forehead had rested there many times after the games were over for the day and they were all napping on the mattress. It seemed so far away. It seemed another world. Things that had happened in another dimension to someone else. Strange: even if you know the smallest details of a body, you can never, ever share the secrets of the person living in it. Greta's body was a picture book, the pages turned a thousand times, words underlined, words read out loud, memorised; but her thoughts, her heart, were a foreign world, far away. Martina didn't know that world, didn't know the customs, the language, the roads and paths carved into endless, unpassable terrain.

Greta talked and talked, smiled, shook her hair, looked Martina directly in the eye and didn't flinch. But she would never touch her, here, in front of everyone. What had happened between them didn't linger in her eyes. It had disappeared – or had never been there.

Mirko arrived, raising the dust with his scooter. He squealed to a stop a few inches from their bench. His eyes were hidden behind big, dark sunglasses. He didn't say anything, he just nodded his head, curt. Martina jumped up – a soldier of the flesh commanded by a gesture. Greta hesitated, but only for a moment. Martina was already on the back of Mirko's scooter, her hands gripping the rack behind her. Then Greta climbed up on to Luca's black scooter and they all left together.

The land was yellow now and the sky was a cloying blue. Smurf-blue – like that horrible new flavour of ice cream.

It seemed like masses of time had passed inside the shed, even though it had only been days. Ten days. The edges had blurred in ten days, things had been forgotten. Their ways, their rhythms, the right way to start. There was no pleasure, just embarrassment, and even some anger.

Mirko began with Greta – which had never happened before. He took her in his arms and threw her on to the mattress like a sack. She protested weakly. Across the room, the others tried to take off Martina's dress and she fought them, biting and kicking. Her eyes were glued to the mattress, to Mirko, to his mouth locked on to Greta's tiny chest, to his hand prying open those thin legs, tearing at her knickers. Then Mirko suddenly stopped and looked over at them gravely. He nodded his head, and Luca took his hands off Martina. Both boys stopped touching her. They went over to the mattress and began pulling objects out of their trouser pockets and their backpacks. Rope, hooks, half-burned candles, magazines, nails, a plastic hammer, a bottle.

Greta burst out laughing. They all did. All of that junk, like years ago when they built model ships with scraps left over in Mirko's garage. They started talking and found themselves again. The right rhythm, laughter, the desire. They forgot about the objects almost right away.

★

83

Sometimes, Martina would wonder if Mirko had ever been with anyone else. She didn't always understand why he'd want to hang out with little kids instead of kids his own age, or even with the older kids. The weirdest thing was that he never talked about the girls who hung out in the yard with his group of friends. The looks those girls gave him were so different from the way she and Greta would look at him. They moved differently, too, their smiles and the way they talked to the boys were different.

Mirko seemed profoundly alone. It was as if something in him suddenly withdrew when someone got too close – he retreated into a hidden, incomprehensible place. He was a liquid substance, sucked out of his body and sunk into a deep hole. When that happened, even his narrow eyes went pale, as if they'd been turned off.

He can barely remember how it was four years ago. Confused memories: the blue, mountain bike frame hanging on his bedroom wall, the Indian tent in the corner. When he was ten years old, he was already the captain of a group of ten-year-olds, yelling at, stomping on anyone who got in his way. He doesn't yell any more. He speaks softly, his voice dry and sharp, like a blade sliding across, cutting skin.

Even when he was younger, there had been those mornings when he woke up . . . not right. But now he woke up like that almost every day. The room was dark and the numbers on the alarm clock burned into his eyes. He always had an erection and he hated that. Once, a friend of his had explained that all men did first thing in the morning. That was a long time ago, before it had happened to him. Back then, it had seemed like a good thing. A symbol of omnipotence. Now, the memory of wanting it was fuzzy and distant. His erections bugged him. He felt trapped. A prisoner. It was the same every morning: wake up and feel it there, standing to attention. It determined everything else. Always. It made him angry and he didn't know why. Sometimes that sense of entrapment turned into hatred and meanness.

So when Matteo had come to him for explanations, he'd answered angrily; he was rude and scornful.

You don't have anything to worry about with that little prick of yours. If it happens to you once or twice in your whole lifetime, you'll be lucky. Stop harassing me. I have other things to think about today.

Before. Before this summer. Before the shed. Before the photos and all the rest. There was this one time he was walking by the wooden frame of a house under renovation and had seen a shadow in ambush behind the boards. He had heard a whisper.

Kid, cute kid, come closer, come on . . .

He had kept walking, trying to get past, but when he was almost beyond the shadow, it pushed something through the boards, a damp, squishy protrusion, rubbing helplessly against his arm.

As he ran away he had tripped and fallen. He ran, ran and turned his head to see if the shadow was following. When he got home, he washed his arm, scrubbed it with soap and a sponge until it bled.

Then. Before that. There was an older girl from school. He was twelve. She was the sister of one of his classmates. She was eighteen. She kissed him on the mouth –

85

unexpectedly – in the middle of a birthday party. In the dark. The candles on the cake had just been blown out. She used her tongue. Amazing. Incredibly amazing. But then so much time passed before it happened again. Too much time. And by the time it happened, he had already turned mean. Girls wanted it and they didn't want it. They showed themselves off with their miniskirts and dirty language and then they pulled away, said no. Look but don't touch. If he'd been persistent they might have softened up after a little while, but Mirko had no interest in waiting. It was all an act. He knew they wanted it, but just didn't want to act like sluts. If he could only just slap them and end the whole performance. They were cows and cockteasers and he didn't have time for that bullshit. His head was always exploding with lightning – violent, percussive bursts. He had to move fast, learn everything.

It was different with Martina. She made him feel neutral. Martina didn't play, she didn't provoke and then run away. She didn't provoke at all. Martina was easy to understand. She was a child. A child who kept quiet: rather than ask questions, she tried to understand things by watching. He liked that about her right away. She was quick to learn. And she was never shocked by anything. Whatever you told her to do, she'd try to figure out on her own. You could tell that, at home, she didn't ask many questions about what you were supposed to do or not to do. They let her do more or less as she pleased. There were only three or four essential rules: bed at ten, do well at school, don't leave anything on your plate and keep your room clean. The end. It was the same at his house.

★

86

One evening, climbing the stairs of her building, Martina saw who Mirko was with when he wasn't with them.

She had gone down to throw out the rubbish, like she did every night and, coming back up, two stairs at time, breathing heavily, she came to the landing and glanced out of the window. She saw these giant shadows moving slowly over the wall of the building opposite. She watched the shapes for a moment, intrigued, the wavering shapes, intertwining with each other, shooting out from a cone of light coming from the bright headlights of a white car parked on the street, smack up against the pavement. They seemed like slow-motion cartoons or Chinese shadow puppets. They wove together, getting bigger: three human figures bound into one single gigantic body. Frightening, like a dragon.

Her gaze wandered down, to the owners of the shadows. One of the three was Mirko. His hands were in his pockets and he was kicking the ground with one foot. He seemed nervous. The other two were much older. They might have even been thirty – almost as old as her father. Even from far away she could see that: from how they moved, from how they were dressed.

They were talking together and gesticulating. The shadows on the building flattened out until the edges were lost and then, in a moment, became defined again. One of the two men stretched his hand out toward Mirko and stroked him awkwardly on the cheek. Mirko jumped away. Then, the other guy handed Mirko a bag, gleaming white under the street lamp and the brightness of the headlights.

They climbed back into the car, slamming the doors shut in unison.

Mirko stood there watching the car pull away. The last shadow, his shadow, slid down the wall and became just a silhouette of Mirko under the yellow light of the lamp-post.

Martina went back inside.

She saw the guys from the white car again after that. They'd appear and disappear. Once she saw them in a bar near the supermarket, sitting on plastic seats under the awning. They were both wearing sunglasses and the white car was parked in front of them. Mirko was seated at the table, too, his hands perched on his knees as if he were about to get up. One of the guys had his hand on Mirko's shoulder to stop him from leaving.

When she turned back, there was no one there any more.

14

For the festival of San Lorenzo, Paolo took them to the canal to watch the shooting stars. Both Greta and Martina's mothers had given them permission to stay out. Luca's mother had, too. Matteo's mother was the only one who said she'd prefer if he didn't go. So Matteo watched them leave from the wooden bench in the courtyard, an angry look on his face. They all squeezed into the back seat of the car. Luca and Martina were crammed next to each other, and Greta sat on Mirko's lap, with her head pushed up against the roof. Paolo's girlfriend was sitting in front and rolling a joint. There was the sweet smell of the hash warmed by the cigarette lighter and the clinging perfume of vanilla air-freshener, which Martina had always associated with the smell of a chewed-up sweet. When she was little, she used to be convinced that someone had spat one out in the car and then lost it.

It was strange to be speeding along in a car. To drive, drive alone, thought Martina, would have been even more beautiful. Sometimes she imagined herself grown up. She pictured herself with long hair, blowing in the wind from the open window of a speeding car, at night. The silence of the countryside and the enormous stars hanging low in the dense sky, so close they almost touched the fields.

But this was beautiful, too. Her head spinning, a circus of colours between her temples. Her shoulders tight up against Luca's, the music, and the reflection in the rearview mirror of Paolo's almond eyes – so much like his brother's. Bright and empty.

Paolo and his girlfriend were talking, but she couldn't hear what they were saying from the back. The speakers were blasting Motherlove; a song that says save the children, with a chorus of children singing in the background.

They all sat with their heads back against the seats, watching the brilliant black countryside rush past the open windows.

Paolo was taking them to a place, past Budrio, toward Medicina, in the middle of the country, where there was a bridge over an artificial canal. A bridge in the middle of the countryside, in the middle of the plains, spanning the nothingness. The profound silence was occasionally disrupted by distant reverberations. Television towers glimmered red and car lights flashed somewhere far off.

They got to the bridge by following an unsurfaced road. The gravel spat out under the car wheels. The bridge was short and wide. It had a low railing and, on the other side of it, the fields began again immediately. It was a bridge between nothing. Useless.

The water underneath was luminous black. Tiny, even waves broke the surface and lapped against the cement sides. Paolo and his girlfriend stayed in the car to smoke and listen to the radio. The music flowed out from the open windows and disappeared into the countryside.

They all sat with their legs dangling over the edge of the bridge and their arms resting on the first rung of the railing, which was just like the guard rail on a steep road. They didn't talk, but fixed their eyes on the sky. A greyish patina of cloud swept over the dark-blue background. There were no stars.

They waited for their pupils to open, to get used to the dark so they could see the animals around them. They could make out the outlines of hares, hidden in the bushes along the edge of the canal, and hear the gentle rustling before the hares leapt out and flew away into the fields with supersonic speed, their long ears pressed back, trailing behind them like scarves.

Luca threw stones, trying to hit them, but couldn't predict their trajectory. The hares would run in random zigzags, suddenly changing direction without hesitation. They fled across the fields, their paws beating the dry earth. The grass shifted around them. Miniature horses, without hooves.

'Why are you throwing stones at them? Leave them alone.'

'Why should I leave them alone? They're idiots, hares are . . . They are the stupidest animals. When a car's coming they wait until the lights are really close before they cross the road. They run right under the wheels. They don't understand anything. Cats are more careful . . .'

'So you want to kill them?'

'Whether I do it, or someone else, what's the difference?'

'There's no difference. But it'd be better if it were no one.'

'Have you ever heard a hare getting squashed under a car? When it hits the bumper it makes a sound like a body falling. First there's this big thud, then a kind of squish. It's gross.'

'Stop it.'

While Luca and Greta talked and teased each other, Martina reached out her hand to touch Mirko's knee and left it there, without moving it. He sat motionless, looking at the black water of the canal, the end of his cigarette lighting up his nose and mouth.

Luca and Greta were shoving each other, pretending to push each other into the water. They fought quietly, without making any noise, without saying anything. Martina looked over at Mirko's mouth again, then, suddenly, she kissed him and buried her nose in his neck.

It wasn't very hot although it was the middle of August. There were no stars and no heat. Just the buzz of angry mosquitoes swollen with blood.

Mirko didn't move. Out of the corner of his eye, he tried to figure out if his brother and the girlfriend could see them from there. He flicked his cigarette into the canal and suddenly got to his feet.

All this countryside around them and the lights of distant cars cutting the field into long strips. Stripes of white, foggy light. It would be incredibly muggy the next day judging by the colour of the sky.

Martina followed Mirko over the bridge. She walked slowly, keeping her eyes glued to the shape of his back as it disappeared rapidly into the darkness. He stopped abruptly, right in the middle of the field. Paolo's car had moved up on to the bridge and the doors were open. The green and red lights from the radio made it seem like a space ship.

They didn't say anything. They faced each other in silence, like two gun slingers, waiting for the other guy to make the first move. She did. She made the first pass, lunging at him. They rolled over the ground. They kissed. That was all. Martina's heart pounded, and she thought how different this time was from all those other times. It was the first time they were really kissing. Then Paolo whistled. It was a shrill, long whistle: a stadium whistle.

When they were climbing back into the car, Mirko grabbed her hand for a second and squeezed it.

They drank before heading home. Paolo had brought wine – red, fizzy, sweet-sour. Fake wine, from a box, that splashed into the paper cups and stained your lips and left your tongue blue.

Greta drank three cups of wine in a row and then felt sick. Her eyes turned bright as if she had a fever. She ran out of the car and leaned against the railing at the base of the bridge, facing the field. She doubled over suddenly, her head launching forward and her hand over her stomach. Vomit: a fleeting red arch. And the sound of liquid hitting the grass. The others laughed, kept on laughing, still sitting in the car with the doors open and the cups in their hands.

There was a dark red stain on Greta's white shirt, right over her chest, in the shape of a heart.

Just a little while before, in mid-August, the town had held its annual party. It was set up in the main square in front of the police station. The stalls filled the air with the heavy smells of sandwiches and french fries. The aroma of cooked

93

oil was everywhere, mingling with the smell of caramelised sugar from the almond-brittle. There was a candy floss stall, too, a flash from the past.

They had built a tiny stage in the middle of the square for the band. The whole town was there: young and old alike, couples arm in arm, the old people with their canes. The night wasn't too hot, there was a light breeze, like just after a rainfall. The songs the band played were out of date, but not too old. Songs from about five or six years ago, that seemed like they were from another century – words and tunes long out of fashion, songs that triggered an ephemeral nostalgia for summers past, parties from other years, other friends. A passing nostalgia, brief, fuzzy, unpleasant.

Mirko, Martina, the whole group, and five or six older kids, sat in the small park behind the ice-cream truck. They ate potato chips from a paper bag in the dark, in silence. They all shared the same gigantic cup of Coke, filled with ice cubes. The speakers from the town square played random, noisy music and they countered by blasting Oasis on Mirko's ghetto blaster. They all sang together over the singer's lulling, grating voice. Tuneless: nobody ever seems to remember, life is a game we play.

Bored but vigilant, it seemed like they were waiting for something. The older ones smoked a joint, blowing the sweet smoke up towards the treetops. Martina sat near Mirko, her head resting drowsily on his shoulder. Matteo sat on her other side and, as she swung her legs, her calves brushed against his. Matteo was sleepy too, as usual. His blue eyes closed and then opened again, slowly.

Suddenly a burst of fireworks shot up over their heads. Big and luminous in the black, star-filled sky. The lights dropped right toward them – spreading out like oil stains. Orange swirls, edged in white, a flood of blue and red, green and purple. The circles in the sky spread, joined together and then faded. The explosions shook the earth making waves in the night air.

They sat with their mouths hanging open, suddenly happy with the summer, the fresh air, being there, still all friends, still the same – after everything. Not doing anything in particular, just existing, peacefully, in the middle of the frantic shouts of children in the square, the laughter of couples walking together down the road, the music, the confusion. Martina squeezed Matteo's finger, smiling.

Ten years old, both of them. So old.

15

Fields outside full of sunflowers. The peculiar colour they turn in the late afternoon under the retreating light and fat, late-summer storm clouds. Pale green stalks and dark yellow, lowered heads. They're like little men, heads folded in exhaustion over slender necks. You can't see their faces. They'll turn black in September. Sunflowers always go black in September, as if burned. Funereal fields spread out under a pale sky.

Martina sat on the mattress. The door in front of her was open on to the fields. A cool breeze blew into the room and caressed her naked skin. Matteo's blond head rested on her stomach, his shaved hair scratching her like the minuscule prickles of a porcupine. His eyes were closed. Two perfect half-moons, rimmed with tiny pink veins, little branches. His small mouth was parted to reveal the whitest teeth. Martina stuck her finger into his mouth, pushing all the way in, sliding her index finger along the cutting edge of his teeth, brushing her fingertip over his tender gums, palette, tongue, until he started coughing as if he were choking and woke up. Then Martina leaned her head into his, holding his cheeks between her hands. He looked into her eyes without smiling. She drew her lips close and kissed him softly. His arms raised up to squeeze her thin, narrow shoulders, the back of her neck, and he hugged her tightly.

They were all lying on the big mattress, their bodies close together amid disorganised sheets and discarded clothes. Mirko's arm was up over his eyes and his shorts were undone. Greta slept on his leg, curled up into the hem of the sheet. Luca was at the foot of the bed, his head lolling off the mattress, his arms hanging down to the floor. Everyone asleep except for them.

Martina looked at her red combat boots tossed into a corner of the room. One of the laces was frayed. She thought of her father. Her father had bought those boots for her. One Saturday morning in December. He was in a good mood and had taken her with him to Bologna. They walked across Piazza Maggiore, hand in hand, like hundreds of other fathers with their children. They watched the pigeons flutter from one side of the square to the other and ate chips from a paper bag, warming their gloveless fingers on the bag. He said he wanted to give her a present, something that she liked, that she had been wanting. In a shop window on Via Indipendenza, Martina had seen, out of the corner of her eye, these little-girl boots, fire-engine red with blue laces, fat rubber soles and round toes. Those, she said and her father bought them.

As soon as they left the shop, her old shoes in a box, the new ones on her feet, she caught her reflection for a fraction of a second in a window and worried that sooner or later her feet were going to grow, and then she wouldn't be able to wear them any more.

16

Out of nowhere something changed – again. An imperceptible shift: a derailment. It wasn't clear whether it started in one of them and then spread to the rest – like a contagious virus – or if, like a fever, it grew within all of them simultaneously at the same pace, as if they were a single organism. A fat compound heart, beating at its own violent, unstoppable rhythm.

There had been a kind of redefinition in the internal hierarchy. Mirko had loosened the parameters of his power, then reined them in again, instituting new variations in the game. But the others hadn't resisted, hadn't challenged him. They didn't even seem surprised, accepting the fact that their acknowledged leader would reassert himself. It wasn't to do with passivity, but simply that Mirko's changes were things they would have got to anyway, a necessary evolution.

The silence inside the shed was palpable. The ghetto blaster was turned off. They all sat on the mattress, neither moving, nor speaking. They waited. They were waiting for Mirko to do something. It was obvious from his expression that something was different this afternoon. Something they hadn't planned on was happening, something new. Mirko opened his backpack and tossed a bundle of magazines on to the bed. When the bundle landed, it made a sharp, violent sound, like the cracking of a whip.

These magazines were different from the ones they'd been using up until then – really different. Some were ironic – people dressed like clowns in leather lingerie, studs everywhere and whips in their hands. Their expressions were playful and a little blank. A few of them were trying to look mean, but you could tell they were faking. But one of the magazines stuck out from the rest. With a flick of his wrist, Mirko slid it to the top of the pile. Smaller than the others, it was black and white, sober, as if it were trying to go unnoticed.

They turned the pages in silence. There was nothing to say. Greta squinted because she was sitting at the foot of the bed, over by the wall, and the others were blocking her view. Martina sat in Mirko's arms, between his legs, her shoulders propped up against his chest. There was a slap of sweaty skin every time she moved.

The photos were ugly, overexposed or too dark, grainy. Like photocopies of photocopies.

No one had ever asked Mirko where the magazines came from, but the question came up this time, spontaneously.

Mirko didn't answer. He lit a cigarette, pulling it from its pack with his teeth and blowing smoke up into the air. A blue spiral rising toward the open window.

The first photo: a man, about thirty, thirty-five years old, his hands bound with rope tied to a hook, his arms raised in the air. There was a whale harpoon stuck into his stomach and a long, thin nail coming out of the hole in his penis. His eyes were two empty orbits.

A man: also about thirty, his scrotum nailed to a wooden board and his foreskin sewn up with a thick nylon thread.

A woman: not very young, not even very pretty, naked, her wrists tied, sprawled face down on the ground, her hair wrapped around her neck and an object jutting out from between the cheeks of her bottom. The object, thin and long – a cane, maybe – it was hard to tell.

Then, there was a series of pictures. The section was entitled, Branding. In the first photo you could see a woman's back. Her arms were tied over her head with a rope attached to the ceiling, her legs were spread, balancing on ridiculously high heels, her bottom offered up to the lens, dead centre. A perfect, white bottom, shaped like a mandolin. To her left, there was a man on his knees wearing a hood. His muscular arms were holding a tool that looked like a giant stamp. He was leaning toward the curve of the woman's arse.

The hooded man was gone on the next page, along with his muscular arm and gigantic branding tool. The picture framed just the woman's burnt arse. Her skin was swollen and red around a picture of a rose with thorns. Her flesh cooked, the colour of raw steak.

There was another black and white magazine in the new bundle. This one had beautiful pictures – the bodies smooth and tanned, the poses languid, sensual. They were children, children like them. Children running on a beach, jumping in the tide, leg muscles taut and glossy with sunscreen, skin smooth and soft, hair tousled. Little girls stretched out on the chalk cliffs – cliffs riddled with holes from the beating of the waves. They looked right at the lens, their eyes deep and wide open. They didn't smile. Their pelvic bones jutted out from their narrow hips and the tight skin over their stomachs. The pictures were peaceful, timeless. The children seemed like exiled sea-nymphs or forest-fairies – just like them, but different.

They leafed through this magazine without too much interest or conviction. There were other photographs stuck in the back, stapled in between the last two pages. These were pictures of children, too. Some of them were very young. The photos weren't pretty like the preceding ones. They looked more like the pictures from the other magazine. They were dark and underexposed. Shadows bit into the children's faces and made them frightening. There were no adults in the frame, but you could feel their presence. They were there, all around, beasts of prey, talons already planted deep into the flesh of their victims. Children tangled up in each other, boys dressed as girls, girls dressed as boys, made up, hands grabbing skin, mouths full of body parts, fingers, genitalia, hair. They handled objects: dildos, bottles.

While they were looking at these pictures, Mirko suddenly remembered something the old guy had said, the one in the white car. He was always kidding around, pretending he was younger than he was, reckless, ready for anything. He made Mirko feel uneasy, bugged the shit out of him sometimes.

'If you and your friends want to do some photos, no big deal, like a game. Just a couple of shots. You could make some money off it . . . You wouldn't mind that, would you? Some money in your pocket?'

Think about it.

Sure, he could do it. He wouldn't even have to say anything. He'd just take the pictures, no warning, and that would be that. It would be a betrayal, but they wouldn't understand it anyway. They certainly wouldn't challenge him on it. Not him. Some extra money was always handy. How would a couple of photos hurt anyone anyway?

After those magazines it was never the same. They let things slide for a while. The yard was deserted. Mirko went away for two days without telling anyone where he was going. Martina got a fever. Greta went off to the seaside.

It wasn't for long. Less than a week later, they were all back in the shed – even Greta. Her grandmother had been ill and the whole family came back early.

They started from the beginning, as if the last magazines had never existed. They tried the same games they used to play, the simple, familiar ones. But there was something off, something they couldn't articulate. A muted lie. They weren't the same as before.

The afternoon they started up again, Greta was acting weird. She complained about being hungry, then sleepy, then bored. She complained continuously until Martina started kissing her neck softly, the way she liked, and she calmed down, as if hypnotised.

They tied her up. Martina did it, under Mirko's direction. The other two stood and watched. Greta laughed, she said she felt like a sausage, the rope all wound up around her legs and hips. But she stopped laughing when Mirko came over and pulled the ends of the rope in tighter. The knots were too tight and her skin was already getting bruised and itchy. There was an army of ants crawling over her, gnawing at her. Her head was spinning. They wrapped a rope around her neck too and her breathing slowed. She drifted off, abandoning herself to the mattress.

They left her like that, stretched out on the bed with her calves tied up and her wrists locked in handcuffs. There was red candle wax melted over her neck and stomach and her skin had turned red and blotchy. Martina was gagged and Luca stood over her gripping her hands to keep them still. Mirko stood at the head of the mattress, a cord wrapped around his right hand, his left hand holding the loose end, like a whip.

It was fun for a while. It wasn't serious; they even laughed. Later, wrapped in Mirko's arms, her hand between her legs in the secret spot, Martina played that familiar game, the game that finished with two or three powerful gushes and a pounding heart. Her sharp teeth left a red mark on his shoulder. A perfect half-moon.

Then they all went quiet, stood up and started to put everything away: ropes, candles, handcuffs were tucked into Luca's bag and hidden behind a chest of drawers. They said goodbye outside the main door of the apartment block, and didn't make any plans.

At the other end of the field the sun was already down.

17

Mirko was wildly off balance the next day. As soon as he got to the courtyard, he started giving out direct, brusque orders. Luca had to go and get a bag of stuff Mirko had left in his garage. They'd meet after at the shed. Matteo listened in silence, then headed off down the road on his bike, pedalling slowly and lazily. The road was so long it would take a century to get there, even if he went at top speed.

Shaking his head nervously at the delay, Luca swerved off, Greta on the back of his scooter, clinging to him.

Martina kept quiet, too. She knew that when Mirko was in this mood, it was best to keep silent and not even look at him. She lowered her eyes and climbed up behind him, resting her hands on his hips even though they were going so fast she felt like she was being pulled backwards by a gigantic rubber band and she was scared of falling off.

It was even hotter inside the shed than outside. Mirko got undressed right away and, with a cool motion of his index finger, signalled that Martina should take off her clothes too. He felt weird, maybe because of the heat, maybe because they were alone and didn't know what to say. He moved closer to her and for the first time he felt apprehensive.

He made her turn round and he stroked the curves of her body absent-mindedly, an electric wave coursing through his nerves.

A little girl's body is different from a woman's. They're both female, but it's not the same thing.

Mirko ran his fingers lightly over Martina's back. From behind, she looked like a boy, with her narrow, sunken hips, tiny bottom, and muscular legs. Her back was long and straight. Only one detail in the middle of her body made her different – in front, a thin, smooth opening instead of a lump of pendulous, sullen pink flesh.

Mirko's knuckles are big and bony. They have deep, dark wrinkles. His whole hand is dark. It always seems tanned, even when his face is pale.

His fingernails slid slowly over Martina's skin, over her smooth back, her shoulders, her arms. They left white marks that quickly disappeared. Pale reddened stripes remained, but they'd be gone the next day. Until the white faded, it seemed like there were loads of pale worms running over her skin, mute and slow.

Mirko watched in silence, concentrating on the design his square nails were drawing on Martina's skin. He lost himself in it. He felt like he was moving through her skin into her body, to the tendons, the muscles, into her blood, her heart, the quick pulsations and contractions.

Matteo still hadn't arrived on his bicycle. Some days he just didn't have enough stamina and he took for ever to get there.

Luca was outside with Greta, unloading the stuff from the scooter.

He could be different when it was just the two of them. Mirko and Martina. His meanness deflated. He softened somewhere inside. He lingered there, neutral and empty, as if standing before a natural landscape too big and majestic to comprehend in its entirety. It was like something he'd seen in a movie, something his older friends had told him about: a man and a woman. Okay, a boy and a little girl. Anyway, it was too deep and delicate to deal with.

His fingers slid over the smoothness. He stared at the corner of the shed – empty, even his head seemed empty. There were just his fingers, touching a child's skin. He didn't want anything. He had no desire to take her, to have sex with her. He wanted the contact. Like petting a dog or a cat, any animal that was sweet and indifferent. Was he bored? It wasn't exactly boredom, but when he woke from this kind of coma, he felt bad. Or rather, ill. His energy was gone. He had to feel mean again in order to bring it back.

Greta and Luca entered suddenly, no warning, no noise. The door swung open and the light slipped in, dense and nauseating with heat. The smell of rotten grass and dry sewage flooded the room.

Mirko pulled his hand back suddenly, as if he had been caught stealing. Martina didn't do anything, she didn't even turn around.

'So? How fucking long is it going to take Matteo to get here?'

His voice came out unpleasant and cold. Mean. It was better that way.

'And you two, did you unload all the stuff? Even from my scooter? Did you get the white bag from the handlebars?'

Greta and Luca stood there, mouths open. There was nothing in the pact about him having Martina to himself, without telling anyone. What was it supposed to mean? Wasn't he the one always going on about them staying together as a group, that they had to do everything together, and that they shouldn't even think about forming couples?

There was this metallic quality to his voice that scared them.

'What the fuck are you looking at? You look like dead fish. Quick, get everything ready. No. Not the bag. Give it to me. Don't touch it.'

Luca passed him the bag without breathing and started pulling stuff out of the other bags. New provisions. Two white sheets, slightly torn. A rope. A flashlight.

Matteo finally arrived. His face was all red and the sweat pouring down his neck made damp halos over the monster on his T-shirt. He was wearing one of his favourite shirts. It was half beige, half black. There was writing in big bloody gothic letters on the top part: Death Power. On the bottom part there was a partially-eaten, skeletal face all demon eyes, red and yellow. It was from his collection. When he was little he called them his 'monster shirts'. He had an endless supply. His mother hated them, but they were the envy of all his friends at school. His cousin, who was always travelling, bought them for him.

He'd pedalled leisurely, his head to one side, listening to the slap of the wheels on the smooth asphalt and the gravel spinning out where the road was cracked. When trucks braked near him, his baggy shorts blew up, baring his legs. There was a long, red scar on his right leg where he'd been bitten by a black cocker spaniel when he was five. He could almost feel it burn when the air blew over it. It didn't bother him, he liked to remember how brave he had been. He hadn't even cried.

He might have seemed distracted, his head in the clouds – as his mother always said. In reality, that was how he concentrated – not on the trucks, or the people he passed, but his eyes and ears synchronised to the bumpy road, the changing gradient of the slope under his bike wheels, what was waiting for him at the shed.

Now he was tired, but happy. He was smiling. Everyone else was in a black mood. Scolded and put in their place, humbled.

They drank some water and then Luca rolled a joint. Mirko was the only one who smoked it. The others just watched. There were new magazines waiting in the white bag, rumpled and full of black fingerprints.

At the right moment, Mirko opened the bag and tossed them to the ground in the middle of the shed.

'So, are you up for a game? Go on, look. We're on another planet here. These are the hardest ones ever.'

Everyone was quiet.

Children again. Like the last time. But no forests or streams, no idyllic seascapes. Four walls, a dirty room. Tiny naked bodies, tied up, gagged, injured. Their eyes covered with little black rectangles.

Luca didn't like these photos at all. He preferred the blondes with enormous tits and abundant hair. This stuff here didn't mean anything to him.

The girls looked without making any comment. Greta was bored. Martina was curious, but speechless.

In one of the bigger pictures there was a little girl, their own age, dressed up like a prostitute, with make-up and thigh-high stockings, high-heeled shoes swallowing her small feet. Her legs were spread for the camera. Her hands had been tied to a chair behind her back and her eyes were dark. It was the only photo that didn't have a black rectangle covering the eyes. And that made it different: it was someone. With the black rectangle, the faces all turned into pale ovals of white paper, a chin, some cheek, a profile. If you couldn't see the eyes, though, a human face became just like a figure in a shop window. It had no expression, no pain, no fear. Maybe they put the rectangles there not only so you wouldn't recognise who the child was, but also because fear and pain are only beautiful when they're anonymous.

Martina went closer to look into the girl's eyes. Her pupils were dilated and her eyes seemed dry. She wasn't crying, but it looked like it wouldn't have taken much more to make her cry.

In the next photo, there was a man with the little girl. You couldn't see his face, just his fat hairy hands, prominent belly and enormous prick which he was sticking into the girl. She was crying now. Her lips were bound shut and her make-up was running. The man was between her legs, spreading them wide with his hands. She seemed squashed.

Another photo: a little girl stretched on the ground, her thin body barely covered by a flimsy, short dress – sky blue. You could just see a man's arm, a thick round arm squeezing the child's thin arm, twisting it at an angle that made it seem like it was broken. This little girl's eyes were covered by a rectangle, a white one this time.

The child's mouth was an open hole, her teeth gnashing in the way that animals defend themselves. That was the impression Martina got from the picture – of a small, wounded animal, mortally crushed by a much stronger, more powerful enemy. A deadly enemy. There was no scream coming from the photo, the sharp, piercing scream that the girl's open mouth must have been making.

'What the fuck's up? Doesn't anyone have anything to say? Doesn't it affect you? It's hard, fine, but we're together. There's no problem. Or are you scared?'

Mirko looked at them with a sarcastic smirk on his pale, thin face. It made him look ugly.

'You're not scared, are you? What's there to be scared of?'

It was just weird. Those bodies weren't like the ones in the other magazines. They were like their own bodies. There was no room for fantasy. They were the same bodies that they had themselves, right there, for the taking. What did the grown-ups have to do with it? The man with his fat belly and hairy hands. What were these photos? Who were they for? Were they for them? Or were they for adults? Children and adults can't mix, can they?

They were embarrassed and tried to change the subject, to do something else. None of them wanted to play now. But Mirko unbuttoned his trousers and signalled Greta to come over to him. The expression on her face was resistant, annoyed – like when the teacher called on her at school and she hadn't studied. She let herself be touched:

her hair, her mouth, her shoulders, her stomach, her legs. Mirko spun her around and squeezed her neck in the crook of his arm, his mouth against her ear.

'We're going to do what I say. So you shut up. Okay?'

They all watched silently, worried. Unwinding the rope from the day before off the globe where Luca had wrapped it, Mirko tied her to the chair, her arms behind her back. He forced open her legs, tearing her white shorts down the middle. A little rip in the seam, a shadow of pink skin.

Mirko went on with this for a while, then suddenly stopped. He ran his hand through his sweaty hair and puffed out his cheeks.

'It's hot. It's too hot today.'

They lay down on the bed, semi-collapsed, their eyes fogged with sweat and their skin burning. They stayed there in silence for over an hour. There was nothing to say. But there was something to understand. Something was changing. It was because of the photos. It was like they couldn't laugh any more. They couldn't have fun. The game was a chore, tiring and unpleasant. It was a false life, full of things they didn't feel anywhere inside.

Martina started thinking about an afternoon a year ago. She and Greta had gone swimming together. They were in the pool, laughing and splashing water on each other. Greta had dived down into the water and sprung up again as if an invisible hand had pushed her, her slim body arched up into the air and the water running off her, into her costume, puffing it out for an instant. Those days were dead now. The laughter they'd shared over the fat lady on the chair, spreading cream on to her sausage thighs was lost.

Laughter. If by laughter you could measure the temperature of friendship, then Martina would say that they were all at less than zero. Cold-blooded, like reptiles.

They were quiet. Words were bubbles swollen with saliva floating in the suffocating air of the shed and bursting against the ceiling without making a sound. Martina lay on the mattress with her arms open and her palms turned upward, imagining all these soft, slow bubbles rising to the ceiling, brushing each other but never uniting. They were like that too, they were like those bubbles. They circled each other, but never met. It used to be different. She wanted to go home, go back in time to before this summer, before everything – erase the last months and find herself catapulted on to the pavement in front of her building, still a little girl, all the other children around her, fighting and stealing each other's toys, ripping them out of each other's hands with delirious, deafening screams. Those were simple, comprehensible gestures. Her world. That normal world. Without ugly dreams and dangerous games. But she was here now, on the mattress in the shed, the others around her, pretending to sleep. There were pillars of reinforced concrete where her legs should have been and her head was heavy like a watermelon full of water. Her right hand inched across the bed, walking on her fingertips, to reach Mirko's shoulder. His neck was sweaty, his veins swollen, his hair wet, plastered to his skin. He didn't move. None of them moved.

Mirko broke the silence. His entire body jerked suddenly and he sat up. He reached out toward the disorganised pile of new magazines, then stopped and pulled back. It was a strange gesture, complicated by a thousand hesitations. He finally let his hand drop with a thud, his fingers spread wide, taking everyone by surprise.

'These don't mean shit. Get it? We're fine without them. We can call it quits on the whole thing if you're going to make those faces. I couldn't give a fuck about any of it. You're all bugging the shit out of me, all of you, the way you act . . .'

He got up and started dressing with hurried, angry movements. Martina watched without saying a word, her hand inert, lying motionless where it had dropped when he moved. Her hand felt enormous, as if it were made of stone. And she was all there, compressed and contained in those five little fingers with chewed-up nails.

Mirko could feel the weight of her hand, too, as if were clutching his neck and wouldn't let him get away. Tiny fingers, stuck like splinters under his skin.

Greta and Luca remained quiet, their eyes on Mirko's back. He fastened his trousers, making his shoulder muscles ripple like a swimmer warming up for a dive. Then his rage evaporated. While he was standing there, tightening his belt, pulling the buckle to its usual hole, something exploded inside him and he started laughing. Laughing and yelling all at the same time.

He couldn't. He couldn't leave. He simply wouldn't have been able to. Two months and his life was all here in the shed. The power was here. He just needed to calm down, regain control of the situation. He could do it, of course he could. And he needed to. The impression left by

Martina's hand had already disappeared. There was nothing left, not a trace. He turned back to them, looked them in the eye, one at a time, and then burst out laughing again. And then they did too, along with him.

18

In the beginning, they used a toothbrush. The round handle of a pink hello kitty toothbrush, with a row of pictures of kittens wearing bows on it. It was easy, like with a thermometer. The tender circle of minuscule pink wrinkles opened right up; and the little girl didn't say anything. She laughed and said that was how the doctor used to take her temperature when she was little. She lay still, on her stomach, naked, her legs slightly parted. Everyone crowded around her bottom. Then they pushed too hard. Luca did.

'I want to stick the whole thing in. What would happen if I got the big part in there too? What if it never came out again?'

Everyone giggled, except for Greta. She was hurt and she suddenly turned over. So they stopped. Hello kitty disappeared into Mirko's backpack and a big bag of cheese puffs appeared in its place – a snack to comfort her. For today.

The game continued. For several afternoons that small, intriguing place became the focus for experiments.

Even the boys let the girls put their fingers inside them. They discovered that they were all more or less the same there. In that minimal region of the body, all differences were cancelled out. But they still couldn't understand how such a tight little opening dilated so much that it could accommodate all their different-sized penises. And there was more – according to Mirko, who promised to reveal new secrets to them soon. But, for now, they shouldn't be too curious.

He had brought the camera. It was hidden in his backpack, the film already loaded and ready for the first picture. It was a red camera, the kind you give to children, with an automatic zoom and flash.

He needed something hard to start with. He would pull it out at just the right moment, without explaining anything. Mirko was thinking about the money. It was the money most of all, even if he was scared when he was out in town. The two guys appeared suddenly, when he was least expecting them. And he really didn't want to be caught with his friends. He didn't want them to know anything about it, to understand anything. *He* brought the magazines. He didn't want them to know there were other people involved, other hands in the mix. That he had someone above him, too, the same way they had him over them. And he was scared that the two men might want more. That beside two stupid little pictures, they'd want to watch, to participate. Then it would get dangerous and he'd be right in the middle of it. He tried to stay out of the way, to hide. He'd walk fast with his face turned away. But the two men always managed to catch up with him. The big white car was a stain of liquid light, a confusion in those steamy summer days, like the road seen from a distance, the air wavering overhead, rising from the asphalt and turning into a lake of polluted water. The car hardly made a sound. It was a long sedan with darkened windows and curtains in the back. The guy who sat in the passenger seat was always the first to talk.

They'd pull up alongside, crawling forward to match the speed of his walk. The back-door lock would open with a deadened click and then he'd have to get in. He wouldn't even say hello. That wasn't how it was in the beginning – back then, he'd brag and talk bullshit to them. Now he'd keep quiet, his head bent low, his hands on his knees, eyes to the ground. He'd wait for the hand to offer up the usual bundle of white plastic. He waited for the sneers on their faces just before they unloaded him, with his prize in his arms. He was always worried that they'd say more. He knew it would come some day; it was inevitable. But they were patient, they took their time. It was as if they had a long-term plan and it was all worked out. The preparation was slow, no improvisation: a perfectly worked-out, geometric scheme. But Mirko was scared.

A new magazine called *Japanese Fist*. It looked almost chaste, at least judging by the cover. A close-up on the dark face of a beautiful Japanese girl, her arm resting against her left temple, her fingers closed into a tight fist. Her knuckles were smooth and white. Her eyes were bright, heavily made up, her lips were thin, pale. You could just see the top of her tanned shoulder where she had a bright red tattoo of an ideogram.

It could have been a martial arts magazine. Or a poster

for an action movie – with a reckless and violent heroine who saves the city from nocturnal monsters or the Chinese Mafia. But the photos inside had a completely different mood. In one of the first images, there was the same girl from the cover, seen from the back. She was bent over, her hands hanging down to the floor and you could see her face and shiny long hair between her spread legs. Up front and centre, there was her smooth, slightly flat bottom, cheeks spread. The brown opening in the middle was wet with sweat.

A second girl appeared on the next page. She was similar to the first, but her hair was short and spiked with gel. Like she had little horns all over her head. Her hand was wrapped in a thin blue rubber glove and her closed fist was dangerously near the first girl's arse, now seen from the side, the girl on her knees on the bare floor. White and black ceramic tiles, an optical illusion.

The next photo: the gloved fist stuck between the buttocks. The first girl's mouth open, screaming. The second girl laughing wickedly, her horned hair sticking straight up, demonic.

Martina turned the pages quickly, her heart racing. Curious, disgusted, scared. And then the whole thing seemed so ridiculous. Repulsion and derision passed across their faces. They didn't talk; the music was on loud and the heat was suffocating. On the table there was a giant bottle of flat fanta and melon rind swarming with flies.

Matteo wasn't looking. He lay draped across the mattress, his head resting on Mirko's backpack, his arms spread wide. A green fly with shimmering wings walked over his nose. He slept soundly until the tape ended and the machine turned off with a click. Then he opened his eyes and saw Mirko, his hand stuck between Greta's legs and a hard expression on his face. Martina was watching with bright eyes.

Luca stood next to Mirko, his mouth and nose tucked into his shoulder. The muscles of his arm were rigid, and his hands were deep in his pockets. Greta wasn't saying anything, her eyes were closed and her forehead was covered with tiny drops of sweat. Her left cheek was buried in the mattress, all red and swollen.

Mirko's fingers were digging deeply into the little girl's rear opening. One finger, two fingers, three. Greta was crying now.

Matteo got up and rubbed his eyes. He went over to the others, but didn't have the guts to say anything. The tension was evil; it was a current of energy binding them – vibrant, hard.

Greta kept on crying, but in a submissive, quiet way. Her tears fell on to the mattress. She didn't say anything. None of them did. Mirko's fingers forced themselves violently into the minuscule opening. None of them had ever seen the expression on his face before. It was determined and ferocious, as if he were in the middle of a dangerous operation and had to finish it at any cost. He had started sweating too. Drops fell on to his shirt collar, forming big stains. Matteo muttered something, tried to ask a question, but the words got blocked. It was all blocked, everything except that hand burrowing into a body – separate from them.

Matteo didn't understand why Greta should be the

centre of attention. She had seemed to accept that she was just a necessary cavity. It wasn't like any of them knew why it was her and not Martina, or Luca, or Matteo. It had just happened that way. Now they had to keep up the cruel game. Her tears were an inevitability. But they couldn't seem to sympathise, or make it all stop. Even Martina didn't question it. There they were, hypnotised, watching the progressive dilation of the hole in Greta's body. They watched Mirko's fingers go in and out. In and out. Just that. They couldn't see her face any more. They couldn't even see Mirko's face. Matteo stood still, watching quietly, his legs trembling.

Suddenly, Mirko stopped. He withdrew his fingers, dirty with blood and excrement and ran the back of his hand over his sweaty forehead. He glanced around the room, as if he were looking for something. And his eyes lit up when they came to rest on an object on the table, amid the flies and the melon rinds. Luca followed his gaze and risked a comment. Mirko shut him up with a look and went over to the table, his arm reaching out to pick up the tennis racket.

Greta screamed when the handle went in, forcing, ripping the opening. But her scream was lost in the mattress, her mouth was jammed into it, and only a mute sound came out. A whimper, like the cry of a sick dog.

Just the first part of the handle. Blood oozed from the wound around the opening. Greta was screaming loudly now, and wouldn't stop. Martina was screaming too but she didn't do anything. They all stood there petrified, watching this terrible scene. Mirko twisted the racket, holding it tightly with both hands like a steering-wheel. He angled it up. He wanted the whole handle to disappear into the girl's body.

Perhaps it was Luca who flipped the tape over and made the music start from the beginning again, a pounding, caustic song – a distorted electric guitar, weaving speedy, crackly chords around this voice that said something like, Stretch the bones over my skin, stretch the skin over my head.

The volume was up loud and no one seemed to notice. They weren't noticing anything any more. Luca wrapped a long strip of sellotape around the little girl's head, eyes, mouth, nose, ears. Her facial features were squashed and deformed under the plastic. Matteo and Martina were shaking. The violent, hard current held them tightly, vibrating through them. All the lightness of the game had exploded into a messy, frenetic rage. Then suddenly the tension broke. A movement from Greta was enough: pushing her elbows into the bed, she tried to get up, and she clawed at the sellotape with her hand. She immediately collapsed. And they all collapsed with her. The little girl abandoned on the bed, bloody and crushed – the rest of them, sweaty and trembling.

They remained still for a long time. It seemed like a dream. Their brains kept starting movements that got stuck before reaching their nerves.

Little by little, they started to move again. Matteo was the first. He went over to Martina, hid his face in her neck and clung to her. Then Mirko came over to them and started the whole thing up again. While Mirko penetrated

Martina, Matteo kept holding on to her hand. She looked into Matteo's eyes rather than the ones hovering over her. Then, she suddenly turned her head to see Luca, on her left, stroking Greta – motionless, on the bed, her face buried in the covers, her eyes half closed.

19

They turned Greta over on the mattress. She was pale and her back was covered with red, swollen scratches. No one could remember how they'd got there – they might have already been there from before. One of her nipples was completely sheared from its place, leaving a dark hole, like a bullet wound. They couldn't remember how that had happened either. A bite maybe, or maybe she'd caught herself on something when she was squirming around on the mattress, the handcuffs, or something else lost in the middle of the mess.

The sheet was soaked with the liquid pouring from her body – a dense, dark substance, blood mixed with something else. They couldn't figure out what had happened.

Everyone stood mute around the bed. Mirko was smoking, he hadn't stopped smoking, he must have been on his fifth cigarette. His eyes were hidden behind dark lenses.

Greta's breath was getting really slow, barely perceptible, a sob. It kept getting slower.

★

If they could only call someone . . . get to the nearest house, the one on the other side of the field, the yellow house.

The house with the ceramics? Where they sell vases?

Yes. But then, what?

Yeah, what do we say? How can we explain . . . There's stuff everywhere, the magazines, all this blood, us here inside. Everything we've been doing. No. We can't say that it was a game. Mirko could . . . But then what? What happens next? What will they do to us?

No, no. We can't say anything. It's a mess; it'll be worse if we talk.

Maybe she won't die, maybe she'll be all right now. It's only been a few minutes . . .

But she needs a doctor. Look, look at all the blood coming out of her. How can we stop it?

We have to keep quiet. Quiet, got it?

What's happened here is between us.

We can't explain it to anyone, they won't understand, our parents.

What the fuck do we do?

Martina is on her knees in front of Greta, her hand on hers, like at Christmas, the time with the decorations.

I want to tell you something, Greta, something I've been thinking for a long time, but I never say. You know, there are places, at night, in the fields, where I've thought we should go alone sometime. Where the fireflies go and make a lot of light. Like it's daytime and, even though there's no ocean there, it'll be like we're looking at the sea. A yellow sea of corn, but at night with the fireflies, the corn will turn blue.

Every time I touched you in the secret place, I knew we were made the same and that you liked it better when I did it than when the boys did. All the games we've played, all of us, even this last one, I did it because you were here, too. You gave me courage . . . You were always complaining, but you smiled and I wasn't ever scared because you weren't either.

I never thought our bodies could hurt each other. I never thought there were right things or wrong things to do. They were just things we did, they were our games. Like we were brothers and sisters. Like being grown up, but still little.

And I can't explain it very well, but you shouldn't be so sick, breathe harder, blow your nose, get up, please, open your eyes.

She thought she was speaking but she hadn't said a word. She just knelt there on the mattress. Greta's little hand, her fingernails painted red and chipped, falling limply from Martina's grasp. They sat in silence – she and the others.

I've seen a lot of blood.
What blood?
Mine.
My mother's blood when she cuts herself in the kitchen, chopping greens. Dad's blood when he slips with his razor.
Mine. When I fell off my bicycle and banged my knee on the wall, that broken-down white wall with all the little pieces of cement sticking out.

I had a hole in my knee once and the blood spurted out like water.

The blood that came out of Cristian's nose at school. The big stains on his rolled-up handkerchief. Bright red.

Nero used to come back from his catfights with long, blood-swollen scratches in his fur.

My blood that time I fell rollerblading and I scraped my hands and knees on the pavement.

That's all the blood I've ever seen.

Then there's Greta's.

The blood coming out of Greta is darker than other blood. It's dark brown, almost black. Purple, even. The wounds on her body – red, puffy lines; soft, open cuts.

They all stood in silence. None of them had ever seen a real dead person. They hadn't even seen the corpses of their grandparents when they died. Children are never shown corpses, even if they are the corpses of people they love. Children are supposed to preserve the image of people the way they were when they were still alive and still joining in the games. Corpses are frightening, except for fake ones. The ones in the movies or on television aren't really dead. They're actors pretending to be dead, or maybe they're really dead, but the images flicker past on the flat screen so fast that it's okay. They're unknown bodies. On TV, real corpses are the same as fake ones and they aren't scary.

But Greta's body was there right under their eyes.

While Mirko dragged the body off the bed and across the floor and then rolled it up in the sheet, they saw her arms and legs dangling limp. Even her neck had turned to rubber and the expression on her face was different from how they remembered it. Her mouth was pale and seemed like it was made out of fabric; dry and wrinkled. Her eyes were open but the lids hung down. They could only see a black half moon: half an iris – extinguished.

20

Mirko was the first to emerge from the torpor. He had to do something, move, get out of there. Start breathing again normally, clear his brain. He took off on his scooter without saying a word. He didn't even look back at them.

It was up to him to sort out the mess. He was going to have to take care of everything – just as he had been doing from the start.

He drove his scooter as fast as it could go, his head buzzing with that phrase – the one they used at weddings: for better or worse, till death do us part. What a load of crap. But if it really was death that was parting them, it was up to him to take care of everything – like he always did. Put an end to the whole story. Don't get caught up in the panic. A definitive end, no traces. He couldn't expect anything from them. He had to act like they weren't there any more.

Within twenty minutes he was back with Paolo's car.

No police around . . . hopefully . . . fifteen years old, no driver's licence, and a body in the boot. Anyway, we're in the middle of the country. It's August. There's no one on the fucking road.

Mirko was furious, but he didn't say anything. He put everything inside a plastic rubbish bag – the magazines, candles, handcuffs, knives, even Greta's clothes. He decided to throw away the camera hidden inside his bag, too. Everything. It all had to disappear. They had to forget everything.

The others were silent and still, afraid even to breathe. It was getting late, already past six, time to go home.

Together they wrapped Greta in the dirty sheet. Rolling her up like a salami, taking care not to get blood on the bare mattress.

Mirko lifted Greta in his arms and left the shed. He had turned the back of the car to face the door and left the boot open. He threw Greta and the bag inside as if they were the same: rubbish, junk, stuff to throw away. He loaded Matteo's bike on to the back seat, cursing under his breath when the handlebars slipped and struck his face.

He made Martina get into the car, up front, and turned the radio up to a sustained blast. The sky seemed liquid, all around them. The clouds were low over the fields, half-consumed, falling. Music and heat. The raspy voice of Alanis Morissette at full volume. And I'm here to remind you of all the mess you left when you went away.

The other two followed on the scooter, like a convoy, without their helmets, clinging to each other, their shorn heads bristling in the mushy air. Martina vomited, bending her shoulders over her legs, doubled up, jerking violently. Mirko didn't say a word. The vomit sat there where it had

132

landed, on her knees, pale yellow: spaghetti with butter and white melon.

The other children were in the courtyard and car park. The little ones surrounded by buckets, action men, dolls, balls, as if they were at the beach. The older ones sitting on their bikes or scooters, getting ready to go. It was dinner-time.

Martina got out of the car without closing the door behind her. She didn't say a word, but headed straight over to the fountain, tripped on her untied laces and got up again. A bright red drop of blood slid down her right knee over her calf and stopped on her white sock. She washed it all away: vomit, blood, tears. When she turned back towards the car, the others were standing there, motionless, arms dangling at their sides, their hands curled into fists. Then Mirko said, 'Nine o'clock, here.' Martina heard him, too. They closed the car doors and left in a hurry.

Walk straight through the fields for five minutes, straight to the ditch and then into it, through the nettles and mud. The moon fading in the middle of the black sky. No voices here.

21

That evening was completely unreal for Martina. Climbing the stairs she felt her legs lifting without effort – as if she were only dreaming of moving. Things navigated around her, turning in the air, not making a sound. Everything seemed light, weightless. She felt like she was inside a space capsule, millions of miles from the earth.

An unreal dinner. Her mother was unreal with her flowery slippers; the kitchen table was unreal and the boiled beans and the napkins set in their places. Everything was the same: the transparent plastic salt and pepper containers, the bottles for oil and vinegar with their painted green letters, 'oil' and 'vinegar' – the same, but Martina had never really looked at them before. There was the same old orange lamp, suspended like a flying saucer over the table, and the yellow tablecloth decorated with pictures of enormous lemons. There was the fan, its white blades covered with a film of dirt. The objects, the habits, seemed part of some beautiful lost world. The beans, the napkins, her mother's flowery slippers, the orange lamp – full of affection and significance. She'd hated these things yesterday. But today, how lovely it would be to look at it all and feel peaceful inside. If today weren't today, but different. If there weren't other things in the way, other gestures, other images locked in her eyes. Planted firmly like the roots of an oak tree, like nails in a wall.

Matteo unloaded his bike from the car. It was already late. The sun had gone down and a street light was shining at the end of the road. While he was pedalling, with his cap pulled down low on his head, his hands gripping the handlebars, Matteo looked into the distance, his head turned to one side, watching the red fields speed past him.

His mother was leaning against the railing of the balcony, wearing her blue and white checked apron wrapped tight over her white vest and shorts. She was out waiting for him.

He leaned his bike against the wall and locked it up. He sat on the ground, by the side of the house, where his mother couldn't see him. He held his head in his hands. He couldn't even force a tear. Nothing came out. Not from his eyes or his mouth. He tried, his head buried in his knees, his mouth open, his eyes shut hard. He tried to squeeze something out, but it was all stopped up. He felt like some kind of stone garden gnome.

He mustered up whatever reserves of strength he had left. Be cool, don't give anything away, face composed, eyes steady.

He only had to climb the stairs. It was easy. How many times in his life had he climbed those fucking stairs? Twenty-three steps: the first twelve, turn left ninety degrees, eleven more to the top – steep, a little dangerous.

Let his mother hug him. Smell her perfume of honey

soap, eyes closed, avoid her gaze, sit at the kitchen table, eat.

Calm. He just needs to stay calm, hold his fork in his right hand, jab the pieces of steak – already sliced and lined up on his plate – bring them to his mouth. Calm.

Chew slowly. Swallow. Feel his stomach fill up. Not lift his eyes from the plate. Keep staring at the TV, pretend he is really interested.

It seemed easy, but every bite was blood in his mouth, a mixture of earth and blood, dark mush, exactly like what came out of Greta's body and flooded the sheets.

Eyes glued to the TV. Be strong.

On the screen, a thin black woman contorted herself into a spider, wailing loudly. Her voice echoed wickedly and made him jump in his seat.

Change the channel, local news, record heat in Bologna.

His mother, seated at his side, keeps refilling his plate: carrots with butter, thick mashed potatoes around the steak. Orange, yellow and black. The colours mix. The plate is a palette of confusion.

Tomorrow it will all be over. Tomorrow. Now, ask mother permission to go out for an hour.

'Okay, but make it an hour. I want you back by ten.'

Luca's sister is the only one home at his house. There's an enormous plate of fried potatoes in the middle of the table. It's Ginny's culinary passion. Ginny – Ginestra: what a stupid name. Only his father could have made up a name like that.

It isn't possible that she made all these potatoes for just the two of them. And, yes, within ten minutes, one of her boyfriends arrives. Luca and the boyfriend don't even say hello to each other. Luca sits in his place at the head of the table, since his father isn't there, his plate of potatoes in front of him. One elbow rests on the table, his head rests on his palm. His eyes are closed.

'Are you tired?'

Ginny's voice has no weight. It is just a breath of wind, barely audible through the noise whirling inside his head, between his ears.

'Yes.'

'So, are you going to stay in tonight?'

'No.'

'Where are you going?'

'Out.'

'I get that. With who?'

'Out.'

She stops asking questions. Her boyfriend has lit up a joint and is pouring red wine into two tall glasses. They are laughing. Even their laughter is inaudible. It reaches him over an incalculable distance, making a sound like shards of glass rolling over a smooth floor.

Mirko doesn't have dinner.

He waits, hidden at the far end of the field behind the apartment building, his hand gripping the car keys, his teeth clenched. He thinks about how everything changed so quickly, and how just one movement can make everything collapse.

They were back in the courtyard by nine. Their dark faces mingled with the excited red faces of the other kids who were all off to the outdoor cinema in the elementary school playground. *Travels with Pippo* was the thrilling title of that evening's film. The children bobbed away, a column of marching ants.

Luca and Matteo sat on a bench. Mirko was inside the car, in front of them, sitting in the passenger seat. Fortunately, Paolo had taken his motorcycle to Corsica, and his parents didn't use Paolo's car. It had been left, locked in the garage under the house. They wouldn't notice it was gone.

Mirko had figured everything out. The boys agreed. After all, Mirko was the oldest – fifteen years old. Luca had only turned fourteen two months ago; Matteo was ten. Their shaved heads hung from their slender, boyish necks. But Mirko stood tall, his brown hair drifting over his long face. His eyes tight, cold like the light of a distant star.

Martina stood two steps behind, her hands in her pockets, gazing out over the fields, watching the summer sunset that seemed never to end, that melted over the earth, slowly splitting itself into a thousand orange tongues.

They climbed into the car, the two boys in the back, Mirko at the wheel and Martina at his side. The courtyard had emptied out. The lights of the car projected a dense, spectral light into the fields. They drove slowly, forty miles an hour, without music. The crickets, the dry and repetitive cry of the owl, the whip of the wind like a long whistle through the grass.

They had turned left out of the car park and then left again after the big magazine kiosk in Via Foggiamorta. The countryside was dark and flat. To one side, before the road curved, there was an orderly row of greenhouses sloping out from the road – giant, plastic white earthworms, suspended over iron arches – ghostly in the moonlight.

The cracking sound of the plastic tents, assaulted by the wind, came in through the open windows. Getting suddenly louder. A tense, rhythmic cracking. Dry. They were all silent inside the car. The even sound of their breath was dry, too. Dry breath, the breath of sick people.

Keep going straight on for five minutes, into the fields and then continue on. Follow the ditch for another five minutes, through the mud and nettles, the frogs and crickets. The fireflies, not yet glowing. Or perhaps gone, who knows where. Black sky now, and a distant pale moon. Not the round moon with her motherly, sad face; a consumed moon, its profile sharp and angry.

22

They went all the way to the end of the ditch, to where a new gravel road began. There was nothing around them, no lights, no barking dogs, no cars. The shadow of country villas in the distance. Fields stretched out, black and silent.

They pulled the blue rubbish bag and Greta's body from the boot. The light of the lurid moon shone pink, almost purple, with spots of blue. The car, doors splayed, the dark night, the naked body – somehow even more delicate now than it had seemed when Greta was still inside it. All those marks, swollen dark wounds covering her entire body.

To Martina it seemed that there was nothing left alive. There was nothing that was part of Greta, nothing in this thing that you could recognise as being Greta. But it was beautiful. The colour of her body, although there was nothing human about it, was still beautiful. Like an extra-terrestrial that had fallen to earth in the middle of the plains of the Po Valley, alone and mute, battered by the meteors and planets it had struck as it fell.

They dug a hole, right at the end of the ditch, a kind of cave under the path. First they put the sack in, pushing it towards the back, then Greta. The soil stuck to her open wounds. She was already a bit stiff, but they pushed her arms and legs together, curling her into a foetal position. She was just like a foetus. She was going back to before, before Greta, before life.

The picture in the appendix of the text book came into Martina's head, the part where they talk about reproduction. There was a picture of a foetus, curled up in the amniotic fluid, inside its sack, in its mother's stomach. The foetus was transparent pink. They could almost see the veins under its skin, its blood, and the shadow of its internal organs in formation. Curled up, all alone there inside its mother's body. Suspended in a hot and silent place, far from the voices, far from pain.

Maybe Greta was like that now too, suspended in a nowhere place, the soft earth on her skin, in her eyes, her ears, her mouth. Soft, cool dirt and the underground movement of crickets, cicadas, worms. A silent population making a passage and nourishment of her body.

They rinsed their hands with water from a bottle, and they also drank a swallow each before Mirko poured the rest over his hair. Martina sat on the edge of the ditch, digging her combat boots into the fresh earth. They gathered some twigs and pulled up grass to cover the turned earth. She sat still, her eyes scanning the fields: blue-black silence, no fireflies. An ocean, still and silent. No fish, no voices, no hands waving to you, trying to touch you.

Matteo started fiddling with Martina's fingers. They were sitting on the edge of the ditch with their feet buried in the earth and their bottoms on the wet grass. Mosquitoes and crickets all around.

Martina's hand was limp in his. There was a scar on her index finger, a backwards 'y'.

Matteo held fast to her hand and rubbed his finger over the mark.

Sometimes the scar swelled and itched, the skin around it went red and Martina scraped it along the bottom row of her teeth, hard, to scratch away the irritation.

She remembered how it happened, and she still liked to hear her mother tell the story. They were in the train and Martina, who wasn't more than three at the time, was wrapped up in a fake fur zebra-patterned coat and sitting on the seat: a tiny bundle wedged between her mother and the arm rest. She started pushing it, trying to make it go up and suddenly managed to lift it. The arm rest came crashing down, catching her index finger on a piece of metal.

Her grandmother was there too. The two women were terrified by all the blood and the screaming little girl. They found the conductor and tried to get him to stop the train right there in the middle of the countryside – emptier and more desolate than the moon. At the nearest station, they took her to the emergency room and the train waited while she was being treated.

An indelible memory: the doctor at the station, a gigantic, paunchy man, held her arm and made her dunk her mutilated finger into a glass of boiling water before he wrapped it up tight in a bandage.

Thinking mostly about her scar as she looked out into the distance toward the end of the fields, she asked under her breath, so Mirko and Luca wouldn't hear, 'What happens to cuts on dead people? Do you think there's enough time for them to turn into scars?'

'I don't know. Probably not. They probably just go soft and melt away with the rest . . . There's no time for scars . . .'

She thought that was horrible. Scars tell so many stories. You don't get them on purpose – not like tattoos – they're the memory of the summer day you crashed into the sharp wall, or slipped on the rocks at the beach. A scar is the thin, visible mark that stays like a trophy after a fight. Even scars from operations are good. Martina always liked long scars, like the scar on Captain Harlock's face, or the one on her mother's stomach from some operation – she couldn't remember for what any more.

But a body that melts doesn't tell any more stories. Why does it need scars?

'So Greta won't have scars?'

'I don't know, but I don't think so . . .'

Matteo squeezed Martina's fingertip tightly in his delicate fingers and she pulled her hand away brusquely without looking at him.

'Stop. You're hurting me . . .'

'I'm sorry . . .'

A tear slid down Matteo's face, right by his nose. Tiny and transparent, leaving a trail in the dirt darkening his face, like the slime a snail leaves.

Martina started singing. Her voice rose up soft, pure and strong. It didn't catch.

Who knows what song she sang, maybe none in particular, maybe it was a bungled tune from a TV show, mixed up with something else. Anyway, her song was just notes, no words. A peaceful song, the least pain possible contained inside it, the least possible anything contained inside it. Music. That was all.

The others stood on the path and listened. Even after the song was over, they didn't say anything. They climbed into the car, closed the doors and left. Forty miles an hour, the radio off. The silence of the country and no fireflies.

Straight into the fields for five minutes, then keep going straight, along the ditch, then down into it, through the mud and nettles. Through the yellow and purple flowers, the frogs and the crickets. Keep going straight, follow the outline of the factory on your right, the low wall that cuts the field in two. Keep going straight, until you get to the end.

When the first frosts come, this last stretch will be slippery, especially at night. When it gets really cold, say, at the end of November, it won't be so easy to leave the house at night. To follow this path through the fields, cross the ruts left by the plough, crush the ice with your boots and come to the sea to sing.

AUTHOR'S NOTE

The characters and the plot of this novel are imaginary, but possible. The places are real. (When I go into Bologna, I like to take the road that goes through Granarolo.) They are familiar places where I have watched a lot of children and teenagers on the streets.

Special thanks to Carlo Lucarelli, without whom everything would have taken much longer to happen.